GIDEON'S MARCH

George Gideon, Commander of the Criminal
Investigation Department at Scotland Yard, has his
heavy workload doubled when he is put in temporary
charge of the Uniform Branch for preparations for a State
Visit, when the Queen rides through the streets of
London with her distinguished guests from overseas.
The throbbing life of the crowd, the pageantry, the
thoroughness of the police in trying to make sure
nothing goes wrong, while at the same time an assassin
plans to strike, hit home with tremendous impact.

GIDEON'S MARCH

John Creasey
writing as
J. J. Marric

·BLACK·
DAGGER
·CRIME·

First published 1962
by
Hodder and Stoughton
This edition 1994 by Chivers Press
published by arrangement with
the author's estate

ISBN 0 7451 8640 8

British Library Cataloguing in Publication Data available

Printed and bound in Great Britain by
Redwood Books, Trowbridge, Wiltshire

FOREWORD

THE PRODIGALITY of John Creasey was outstanding. Shortly before he died it was calculated that in a forty year period he had written 560 novels—mysteries, westerns, action thrillers—which at a very rough calculation meant writing one book every 26 days for forty years, which is 1,400,000 words a year, which is around 56 million words in forty years which is why he is in the record books as one of the most prolific writers of all time.

On average he wrote about 12 books a year but in the period 1938-1944 this increased to twenty. His average period of writing was rarely more than ten days, and with five days allowed for revision, each book would take him no more than two weeks. He had no idea what would happen when he sat down to write but simply tapped into his sub-conscious creativity and stepped into his fictional world.

The books are not intellectual puzzles but emotional journeys through a multi-layered text of plot and counter-plot. Part way through *Gideon's March* there is a recapitulation of ten sub-plots still to be resolved yet such is Creasey's deftness that the reader has never lost sight of the individual strands as they intertwine. Creasey concentrates on the basic emotions such as fear, greed, and hate; there is never any doubt as to who are the good guys and who the bad. Creasey's is what would be called nowadays an old fashioned morality. In his world there is always a clear sense of right and wrong, of codes to be followed and standards of behaviour to be observed. The impression is of a safer more secure society in 1962, when the book was published, than the world of today.

Neither *Gideon's March* nor *Gideon's London* attempt to reflect in any serious way the pre-Beatles society of the early 1960's. Consciously or not Creasey was using the sixties landscape as veneer for a society and values that had almost disappeared and for which there were already nostalgic yearnings.

Understandably the book's hero, Commander George Gideon, has to reflect those values which he does in this and other books in the series. In the choice of name Creasey was making a statement as to what some of those values should be. The name means 'breaker' (which Creasey's Gideon is of the underworld) and both are judges, one in the biblical and one in the legal sense. Both are humble men yet mighty men of valour. *Gideon's March* tells you little more than that, although the casual references to the past make it clear that Gideon must have joined the police force in the hungry thirties (1934 to be exact). Did he join from a sense of vocation or was it because he was out of work? What about his wartime experiences either as a policeman or a wartime conscript? There is not a hint about either. Character is subordinate to plot. The little extra we learn about him is that he loves his wife, they have three children, he likes eating meat puddings, gardening, reading Sunday newspapers in the front (best?) room and is domestically competent to mend a window blind. On balance an understanding of the Biblical name has told us more.

Gideon's London is free of towering office blocks and Scotland Yard is still housed in Norman Shaw's turreted streaky bacon building on the Victoria Embankment. All this would change within a few years. Some changes Creasey could and should have recognised if it was the sixties society he had intended. The Police Commissioner was now somebody who had worked his way up through the ranks and not, as in the novel, a government appointee with two former colonial postings. Instead of old fashioned gangsters with razors, coshes and water pistols filled with acid the London underworld was being fought over by gangs such as the Krays and Richardsons. Creasey throughout his work tended to avoid such brutality which, like sex, he found distasteful to write about. Creasey's gangsters are much less threatening. On two occasions the falling crime rate is attributed to the colder weather. Presumably Gideon's underworld prefers to stay at home, keep warm and let crime take a rest! Reality does intrude with the attempted assassinations of the Presidents of France and America. Although both General de Gaulle and

John F. Kennedy are clearly indicated neither is mentioned by name. In the case of the latter it is an uncomfortable foreshadowing of the assassination that was to follow only a year later.

Gideon's March then is not a reflection of 1960's society but of the 1930's society which is when Creasey began successfully writing. This was the world he knew about and one that could best reflect the qualities of the sort of society he believed in and which could be reflected through the character of Gideon of the Yard. When coupled with a prodigality of invention, generosity of plots and sheer readability it was an unbeatable combination.

DONALD RUMBELOW

Donald Rumbelow is a former Chairman of the Crime Writers' Association. He regularly writes and lectures on London history, police and crime especially on Jack the Ripper, a subject on which he is recognised as the international authority. He is a former policeman and qualified London guide specialising in walking tours. His chief interests are book collecting, 19th century prints and the English Civil War. He is married.

THE BLACK DAGGER CRIME SERIES

The Black Dagger Crime series is a result of a joint effort between Chivers Press and a sub-committee of the Crime Writers' Association, consisting of Marian Babson, Peter Chambers, Peter Lovesey and Sarah J. Mason. It is designed to select outstanding examples of every type of detective story, so that enthusiasts will have the opportunity to read once more classics that have been scarce for years, while at the same time introducing them to a new generation who have not previously had the chance to enjoy them.

CONTENTS

1

LONDON'S PAVEMENTS

THE old and the young wives' tale about the pavements of London being harder than pavements anywhere else had never impressed George Gideon, partly because he had long been aware of the usefulness of thick leather soles. In his schooldays and early adolescence, home-made soles had been hammered on to the shiny surface of new boots and shoes by his father, who had been hard put to it to make ends meet, yet determined that no son of his should ever go ill-shod. Soon after he had been accepted by the Metropolitan Police as a constable, and stationed in Hampstead—just about as far away from his home in Fulham as one could get in the Metropolitan area— Gideon had realized the importance of boots, shoes and feet which could stand up to a lot of use. His first extravagance had been to have boots made for him, with specially padded soles; his second had been to pay hard-earned money for the monthly attention of a chiropodist. To Gideon, always a man of down-to-earth common sense, this had been the same kind of thing as making sure that the tyres of his bicycle were inflated properly, and that the tread was never smooth.

A consequence of this was that today, in his fifty-third year, he could pound the pavements of London as solidly and purposefully as any newly appointed constable. Sometimes his legs ached ; his feet, never.

In those early days a glow of romanticism had seemed to turn the smooth paving stones to gold, or the promise of gold, and in a way he had never stopped looking for it, although there was no more rational man in London. Few things gave him more satisfaction than a walk through his own Square Mile, with Piccadilly Circus its heart. London had the comfortable familiarity of a good wife, and gave him just as much satisfaction.

On a morning in May, just after nine-thirty, Gideon got off a bus half-way along Victoria Street and walked towards Westminster Abbey; there were few approaches to London which he liked better. He was on foot because his car was being serviced. A squad car would have picked him up, but he preferred to go by bus, even though it had meant queuing for ten minutes, then standing for another fifteen. Now he strode along, watching the late arrival office workers darting into gloomy doorways and disappearing up narrow staircases or crowding round old-fashioned lifts. This part of London had changed very little in fifty years, none of the rectangular modern blocks of offices and flats yet gashed the skyline. Gideon strode along, head and sometimes head and shoulders above most of the people whom he passed, big powerful shoulders slightly rounded, thick iron-grey hair brushed straight back from his forehead, head thrust forward—he walked as he lived, always knowing where he wanted to go, and finding the shortest way. He had a look of almost aggressive power. Every policeman on the route stiffened when he recognized the Commander of the Criminal Investigation Department.

Two sergeants met at the approach to Parliament Square just after he passed.

"Old Gee-Gee looks as if he'll be on the rampage this morning," one man said.

"I was just thinking about him," said the other. "I've known him for twenty years, and except that he's a bit greyer he hasn't changed at all."

"Dunno that I want him to change," the first man reflected. "Do you remember the time when he said if we didn't get more men on the force, he'd throw his hand in?"

"Who doesn't? Wonder why he's walking this morning?" the second man mused aloud, and grinned. "Probably come to keep an eye on us, although we wouldn't know it!"

Gideon kept to the right of Parliament Square, passing the statue of Abraham Lincoln, so that he could see the courtyard of the Houses of Parliament, Big Ben, all the recently cleaned gothic stonework, the intricacy of the carving, the satisfying, harmonious whole. Then he reached the corner of Parliament Square, glanced along Whitehall towards Trafalgar Square, and made a pickpocket who was having an early session dodge quickly out of sight; there were many habitual criminals in London prepared to swear that Gideon had eyes at the back of his head.

He turned along the Embankment, glanced across at the London County Hall, heard a moaning note from a tug on the river, was saluted by two uniformed men on duty as he turned into the Yard, and up the stairs to the front hall. The duty sergeant said "Good morning," and smiled. A dozen strapping, youngish men were waiting in the hall, and Gideon remembered that a party of Australian policemen from the Criminal Investigation Bureaux of five states were going to be shown round the Yard. The grey-haired sergeant opened the door leading to the C.I.D. section of the building, but Gideon turned round to look at the visitors.

"Is Detective-Inspector Wall here?" he inquired.

A man with a rather big head, and a very brown face, took a half-step forward.

"I'm Detective-Inspector Wall, from Brisbane."

"I'm Gideon," said Gideon, knowing quite well that they had been told who he was as he had walked up the steps. "Glad to see you, Inspector. Your father was a Superintendent here when I was a flatfoot." He shook hands with Wall, and acknowledged the others with a wave of the hand. "Enjoy the tour."

He went through the passage door, leaving a gratified and murmuring group behind him, and strode along to his own office. He knew that from the moment he had stepped into the Yard, old Joe Bell had been warned. Joe, his personal *aide*, was only a few years off retirement, and there were those who said that he should have retired at sixty, not waited until he was sixty-five. He was the best personal assistant Gideon had ever had. Already he would have all the morning's reports looked over and placed in order of importance.

He was sitting at his desk, square behind the door; Gideon's desk was slant-wise across the wide window, so that he could get full advantage of the light from the Embankment. The office had pale green walls, dark brown furniture, a carpet, two filing cabinets, several telephones and a couple of rows of books—from police manuals to bound copies of the *Police Gazette*, Gross on *Criminal Investigation*, Glaister's *Medical Jurisprudence*, a dog-eared dictionary, and a current edition of *Whittaker's Almanac*, as well as of the New York *World Telegram's World Almanac*. This last was a regular Christmas gift from a friend in New York Police Headquarters.

" 'Morning, Joe."

" 'Morning, George."

Gideon eased his collar, then took off his coat; it was warm, and the sun was gilding the windows.

"How have the bad men been behaving?" inquired Gideon, and glanced out. The Thames' boats were gay with striped awnings on the smooth water, for the up-river and down-river trips had already begun.

"About average," said Bell. He was a smaller man than Gideon, rather plump, round-faced, a little untidy, nearly bald, always apparently in need of a haircut. "You'd better have a talk to Abbott. He's got a bit mixed up over the Carraway job, can't make up his mind whether we ought to charge Carraway or just watch him. Apart from that, there's nothing you need worry about until you've seen the A.C."

Gideon, glancing down at some reports on his desk, said absently: "Eh?" and then looked up. "What was that about the A.C.?"

"I had a call put out over the air for you. Didn't you get it?"

"I walked."

"Oh, lor'," said Bell, in dismay. "I thought you'd be

all ready for the conference." He was obviously perturbed. "Something's up. I tried to get an inkling out of the A.C.'s secretary, but the bitch says she doesn't know what it's all about. Can't we do anything about that woman, George? Ever since she got that job, she's been—"

"When's the meeting due?"

"Rogerson says will you go in as soon as you can."

"Where's Abbott?"

"Waiting next door."

"I'll talk to him." Gideon picked up a telephone, said: "Mr. Rogerson, please," and held on. After a moment, he heard Rogerson's secretary. "Mr. Rogerson there?"

"Who wants him, please?"

This was what Bell meant; the newly appointed but fairly long-in-the-tooth secretary who had been wished upon the Assistant Commissioner knew perfectly well who was calling. Gideon was tempted to raise his voice, but instead said mildly:

"Commander Gideon."

"Just one moment, Commander." There was a pause, and during it the door opened and Abbott came in. Abbott was a comparative newcomer to the Chief Super-intendents' ranks, and wasn't yet sure of himself. Gideon had a feeling that he might never make the grade; he was too often afraid that he might do the wrong thing.

"Take a pew, Abbott," Gideon said, and Rogerson came on the line.

"Yes?"

"How long can I have?" Gideon asked.

"Can't you come right away?"

"I'd rather be ten minutes."

"All right," said Rogerson. "We'll turn up a bit late. Don't be a minute longer than you can help."

"I won't," promised Gideon, and put the telephone receiver down and pushed his chair back. He knew that to Abbott, as to many men who did not know him well, he was something of an ogre; certainly a man to be wary and chary of.

Abbott was shorter than many at the Yard, and that

put him at a disadvantage. To look at, he was the ideal strong man of the boys' adventure books; his chin was square, his brown eyes deep-set, his eyebrows thick, well defined, and slightly blacker than his hair, which was beginning to turn from chestnut brown to grey. He moistened his lips.

"'Morning, Abbott," said Gideon. "Carraway playing you up?"

"I can't make up my mind whether we have enough evidence against him to justify an arrest," said Abbott. "Mind you, I'm pretty sure he's our man. But his alibi for the night when Arthur Rawson was murdered might ·stand up. And if it does—" he broke off.

"Seen Carraway himself since yesterday morning?"

"Only for five minutes."

"What did he say?"

"He's as bland as ever, Mr. Gideon—seems to enjoy pretending that he doesn't know that he is under suspicion of murdering his partner. The fact remains that he inherits the business, and he was in serious financial difficulty·before his partner's death. Apart from this alibi, we could make a good case," Abbott said. "There's another angle I'm following up. Carraway's living with a young girl named Belman, Marjorie Belman. I thought she would turn out to be a hard-bitten bitch, but she seems a nice enough kid. I'm going to see if I can work on her to break the alibi."

"Go over it again, every aspect of it. Interview the three men who make the alibi for Carraway, then talk to that girl. Be here at six o'clock sharp this evening, and we'll go over it together."

"I'll be here on the dot," Abbott promised. "Thank you very much, Mr. Gideon."

He backed out.

"If you ever make him worth a Chief Super's pension, I'll buy you a dinner," said Bell. "You going to leave the rest to me?"

"Yes—but keep a check on that Australian party, make sure no one skimps with them in the *Information Room* and in *Records*. Send a personal note—no, wait a minute, I'll do that myself." Gideon lifted his telephone as he got up, and said : "Get me Mr. King-Hadden, of *Finger-prints*." He stood looking across at Bell, saying : "You have a word with the Black Museum, and make sure that they don't overdo the sex and sadism stuff. Hallo, Nick—George here. You know we've an Australian party on the way round ?" He grinned. "I know what you think about Cooks' tours ! Make sure they get a complete story on those prints you dug out of the pot-hole in Derbyshire, will you ? Show 'em that the Yard can solve a forty-years-old murder when it feels like it. And tidy your place up a bit. . . . You know damned well what I mean ! Show one of your chaps a duster, clear away some of the junk in the corner, and don't have too many dirty tea cups around." He paused, chuckled, and went on : "All right, Nick, all right, I'll look in myself and see whether you've had a spring cleaning or not." He rang off, took his jacket off the back of his chair and went to the door. "Now I'll go and see what all the trouble's about," he said to Bell. "I can't think of anything that would need a special con-ference, unless the Home Secretary's latest pronounce-ment on the state of crime in the country has stung questions out of the Opposition. We haven't got any big job outstanding."

"Nothing I know of," Bell said.

"I'll get back as soon as I can," promised Gideon, and went out, thinking of the summons and, a little uneasily, about Carraway.

"And it's got to be done as soon as possible," Carraway was saying, about that time. He was a man of medium height, smooth haired, smooth shaven, with very dark brown eyes. He looked into the scared face of Eric Little, one of his car salesmen, and took a packet of five-pound notes out of the side pocket of his beautifully tailored tan-coloured suit. He slapped the wad on to the palm of his left hand. "Here's five hundred of the best, Eric. You get the other five hundred when she's dead."

"Bruce, how do you know she'll talk? How do you know— ?"

"She'll talk because she hasn't got the guts to stand up to police questioning," Carraway declared. "You know it as well as I do."

"Listen, I—"

"Now you listen to me," interrupted Carraway sharply. "You take her down to Brighton, and drown her. I don't want any more argument. You're getting a thousand quid for the job, you've got nothing to worry about."

"Bruce, Jorrie's a nice kid—"

"So what? There are thousands of nice kids. There was one you strangled, remember? You choked the life out of her because she was in the family way, and going to make trouble with your wife and kids. You got away with that, thanks to me. Now you'll kill this other *nice* kid—my way. Because if you don't, an anonymous telephone call to the police will make them ask a lot of awkward questions. Don't give me that line about conscience."

Little muttered: "Okay, Bruce, okay." He put his hand out and took the wad of notes. Soon, his eyes brightened. "Don't you worry," he went on. "I'll put her down with the fishes." He moved away and looked through the glass walls of Carraway's office, to the rows of used cars, all marked *For Sale*, and at the big sign which read: *Car Hire—Lowest Terms*. There was a slump in second-hand car sales, and it would take him six months to earn five hundred pounds in commission.

Carraway, who knew him well, could almost read his thoughts.

2

SPECIAL CAUSE

THE office of Rogerson, the Assistant Commissioner for Crime, was on the same floor but round a corner from Gideon's. Rogerson was sitting on the corner of his desk, dictating to the middle-aged secretary, a Miss Timson, who had recently taken over from another middle-aged secretary who had unexpectedly decided to get married. Miss Timson was rather tall, slightly angular, always neatly and simply dressed, always freshly coiffeured; except for her manner, there was no way she could be faulted. Her manner now said that even the Commander should have knocked. Rogerson held up a hand to Gideon, and finished dictating:

". . . and in my considered view the Home Secretary's statement to the House of Commons that crime in London is showing marked signs of a decrease is ill-advised and ill-timed, as the decrease in the period under review is almost certainly due to the extremely hard winter. That's all, Miss Timson." He stood up. "Good morning, George."

" 'Morning," said Gideon, and waited for Miss Timson to disappear. Her skirts were short; she had nice legs, and from behind looked ten years less than her age. The door closed on her. "What's the rush?"

"Don't know much about it myself," said Rogerson. He was tall, and running to fat, although when Gideon had first known him he had been lean and hardy-looking. A coronary had pulled him down, and he was no longer allowed to play golf or take much exercise. "Might be this Home Secretary nonsense in the House yesterday. You heard what I think of it."

"Heard an echo of what the Opposition thinks of it," said Gideon, mildly. "That all you've got?"

"Scott-Marle's secretary said something about the Permanent Under-Secretary of the Home Office being with the Commissioner. Let's go."

Gideon opened the door, and they walked out of the Criminal Investigation Department Section, through long, bare passages and past long windows of frosted glass, until they reached that section of the Yard given over to administration. The Commissioner's office was very nearly luxurious, but the Commissioner himself, Sir Reginald Scott-Marle, did not like ostentation. For years, Gideon had regarded him as a very good man at his job, but cold as a fish. Recently he had come to know him better as a person, to like as well as to appreciate him. He had held two Colonial posts before coming to the Yard, and was known as a man who would make no concessions for the sake of peace and quiet.

His secretary was smaller, younger, bigger-bosomed and untidier than Miss Timson.

"You're to go straight in, gentlemen—the Commissioner is here already." She opened the door of the Commissioner's office, and this told Gideon that it was to be a small-scale conference; a large one would be held in the main conference room.

Scott-Marle was sitting behind his large flat-topped desk, looking a little aloof. Charlie Ripple was perched rather awkwardly on a wooden armchair noticeably too small for him. Ripple, the Commander of the Special Branch of the C.I.D. and an old friend of Gideon's, was broader across the beam than most chair makers allowed for. He always dressed in brown, he was more muscular than fleshy, and he had a large bald spot although his hair remained a dark brown; the uncharitable said that he had it dyed. Sitting next to him was Sir Thomas Barkett, the Permanent Under-Secretary at the Home Office, a formal man, a clever man, one who believed in the conventions, in tradition, in propriety—and yet could slash red tape.

"Good morning," Scott-Marle nodded, almost coldly.

"Sit down, please." Gideon waited for Rogerson, then sat well back in a chair the same size as Ripple's; the fit was fairly tight. He nodded across at Barkett. As he did so, the door opened again and Mullivany, the Secretary of the Metropolitan Police, came in, bustling; he was always inclined to hurry, always inclined to bemoan the fact that he never had time to do his job properly. He took the one vacant chair.

"This is a preliminary conference about a task which could give us all some awkward problems," Scott-Marle announced, and looked at Barkett invitingly. "Would you care to give us the details, Sir Thomas?"

Barkett was dressed in a well-cut black jacket, grey striped trousers, a silver-grey tie.

"That's what I am here for," he said. "I needn't take long. The meeting of Foreign Ministers of the main Western States has recommended an early Western Summit, to prepare for early proposals to the Soviet Union. It is to be held in London, and they aren't wasting any time—they want to get it in before the next Russo-Chinese Conference. So there will be a visit to London from the Heads of Governments of the United States, France and Western Germany. It has been arranged for the first week in June—in exactly four weeks' time." He had a rather casual way of speaking, as if he were really thinking of something else.

"The Government has decided that invitations should also go to Heads of States, so as to make the meetings more impressive. The State Visit will be in addition to the political meetings between the Heads of Governments. There will be a State Procession to the Houses of Parliament, where the Heads of States will make speeches at a joint meeting of the House of Lords and the House of Commons." Barkett sounded almost bored.

"The Procession Route will be from the Palace, along the Mall, Whitehall, Horse Guards Parade, the Embankment and Parliament Square, and on the way back will go round Parliament Square, enter Parliament Street, proceed along Whitehall and then through Admiralty Arch and back to the Palace." Barkett paused for a moment, his pale hands resting on a thin, black brief-case on his knees.

"This procession will follow a luncheon at the Palace, and will take place on Wednesday, June 2nd. The Heads of States will arrive in London by air on the Monday or Tuesday preceding. On the Tuesday evening there will be a French Reception ; on the Wednesday they will address a joint meeting of the Houses of Parliament at midday and there will be an American Reception in the evening. The State Visit will end on the Thursday evening, following luncheon with the Lord Mayor of London, and the politicians will then get down to their job."

Barkett stopped.

"Such short notice," Mullivany complained.

"Nice to know someone is getting a move on," Ripple said.

Rogerson remarked, *sotto voce* : "Well, when they're at the House and the Guildhall, we'll have a breather."

It was the kind of inane remark which Rogerson was liable to make occasionally. Ripple glanced at Gideon, and wriggled his rear to get further back in the chair. He had a heavy chin, a rather broad nose, unexpectedly mild brown eyes. He was probably as puzzled as Gideon because Grimshaw, the Commander of the Uniformed Branch, wasn't present.

Scott-Marle looked at Gideon, but seemed to address them all :

"How much of a problem does this give us ?"

Rogerson hesitated, and then said : "The usual main one, I suppose—moving enough men from the Divisions into the West End for the occasion. It always means stretching things a bit." Sensing that Gideon wasn't yet ready for comment, Rogerson went on : "What do you think, Ripple ?"

Gideon was still puzzling over Grimshaw's absence.

"I can't envisage any serious trouble, but you can never tell on a job like this," Ripple said. "Apart from the lunatic fringe, we're bound to get some hot air from the Ban the Bomb boys and girls. Eh, George?"

"Bound to," agreed Gideon.

"I've got reasonable time to get in touch with the people overseas," said Ripple. He rubbed his chin; everyone could hear the rasping. "Have to get cracking, though. Got to check up with the Security chaps in Washington, Paris and Berlin—know what I'd like to do, sir?"

Scott-Marle asked: "What would you like to do?"

"Nip over and see these chaps," answered Ripple airily. "Find out at first hand what kind of precautions they want us to take. Then they can come over a couple of days before the big show and check that everything's the way they want it."

"Is this *really* necessary?" Mullivany wanted to know.

"What I mean," went on Ripple eagerly, "is that if I can have a talk with the chief security chaps who'll be coming with the nobs—I mean the Heads of States—it will enable me to look after my side of the problem properly." He sounded almost smug as he glanced at Barkett. "Don't you think that would make the other States realize we were taking every possible precaution?"

Barkett didn't waste words. "Yes," he said.

Mullivany frowned, but made no further comment.

"When I get back I'll be able to make sure we're on top of the job," Ripple said. Then he allowed himself a grumble, as if realizing that he mustn't show too much pleasure at the prospect of the visits abroad. "Been much better if we'd had one Head of State at a time to deal with, though. These big conferences are hell."

"I think you would be wise to consult with the Security authorities in each of the three capitals," said Scott-Marle. "See to the arrangements, will you?" That was to Mullivany. Then he went on: "Gideon?"

"First thing I'd better do is find out who's out and about the first week in June," Gideon responded slowly. He didn't need to explain that certain kinds of criminals thrive on crowds: the pickpockets, the bag-snatchers, the shop-lifters, the touts, the confidence tricksters, the dealers in forged notes and counterfeit coins. The whole of the Criminal Investigation Department in the Metropolitan area would have to be alerted, and the County and Borough forces, too. The brunt of the arrangements would really fall on Uniform, however, and it remained a puzzle that Grimshaw wasn't here.

They were all waiting for Gideon to go on.

"I'll have to get as much leave stopped in that week as I can, and I'll get busy with all the Divisions." He grinned at Ripple. "As a matter of fact, I think I ought to go and see them all!"

Even Scott-Marle chuckled.

"Going to fly?" inquired Mullivany, half-sourly.

Gideon didn't retort. He had a feeling that the Commissioner still had something important to say.

"Sir Thomas?" invited Scott-Marle.

"I was with the Home Secretary himself last night," announced Barkett, "and he made it clear that he hopes very much that the improvement discernible in the figures for crime throughout the country, particularly in the Metropolitan area, will be maintained during this visit period. You will have all possible co-operation from the Chief of Immigration to keep undesirables out of the country. The Minister asked me whether it might not be possible to use the June visits as a kind of morale booster," went on Barkett. "They were his actual words. If the exemplary behaviour of London crowds when welcoming overseas guests were emphasized, and—"

"See what he means," said Gideon, hardly realizing that he was interrupting. "Prove that the relationship between the police and the public has got right back to normal, and that this relationship is a big factor in the improvement of the crime situation. Is that it?"

"Yes."

"Might not be a bad idea at all," conceded Gideon. He ventured another grin and said: "These politicians occasionally have a good idea, don't they? When I see the Divisional chaps I'll put it to them that we've been given the chance we've been waiting for. There will be a few Jonahs, but there always are. The only thing I can't understand, sir, is—where is Commander Grimshaw? This is largely a uniform job."

"Grimshaw's going to be on sick leave," Scott-Marle announced, and everyone in the room reacted with surprise and near-dismay. "He has had some chest trouble, and the doctors have found a spot on one lung. He should be back in three months, and I don't propose to fill his position. He has a young deputy who should not be faced with the responsibility of such an occasion, so I want you to take charge of both C.I.D. and the Uniform arrangements for the State Visits, Gideon. I know it will mean a lot of extra work for a few weeks, but I hope you'll find that it's worth it."

Everyone was looking at Gideon.

Gideon pursed his lips, smiled wryly, and said : "I hope you find it worth it, sir."

"We must compare notes when all the Heads of States are safely out of the country," Scott-Marle retorted drily.

Gideon left the Commissioner's office, half an hour later, with Rogerson on one side and Ripple on the other. They had left Barkett obviously pleased, Scott-Marle in a better-than-usual mood, and Mullivany silent.

Gideon himself had mixed emotions. A "lot of extra work for a few weeks" was a considerable understatement. He was going to be run off his feet. That prospect could only make him feel uneasy, for ordinary crime would not stop while he got ready for the big show.

His greatest cause for misgiving, however, was nothing to do with the work involved. He wondered what Ray Cox, the Deputy Commander of the Uniformed Branch, would feel. He knew Cox slightly, and agreed with Scott-Marle that he hadn't sufficient experience for the job. If anything went wrong, the Commissioner would be held to blame for having too young a man in charge of the Uniformed Branch. He had made the right decision, but Cox would probably disagree.

"Better let Scott-Marle brief him first, then I'll go and see him," Gideon decided.

He wished very much that he knew Uniform's Deputy Commander better.

Ray Cox said: "I quite understand, sir." He stood stiffly at attention in front of the Assistant Commissioner of the Uniformed Branch of the Metropolitan Police Force, who was an elderly, rather vague-mannered individual with a keen administrative mind.

"That's good," said the A.C. "Doesn't make your job any less important, of course."

"No, sir."

"And I'm sure you'll get along well with Mr. Gideon."

"Thank you, sir."

"Let me know if you run into any problems," the A.C. said, in a tone of dismissal.

Cox said: "Yes, sir," formally, and went out. He was tall and lean, with black hair and an unexpected bald spot which showed up very white, with square, almost angular shoulders, and a long neck. His features were thin, his nose too long and pointed, but his mouth was full and he could smile easily. His eyes were piercingly blue.

He was not smiling as he shut the door, or when he went back to his own office. He was glad that it was empty; he did not feel like talking to anyone. He went across to the window overlooking the courtyard, his hands clenched, his eyes very narrow, even his lips set tightly.

"My God, what do they think I need? A watchdog?" He took out cigarettes, lit one, blew smoke out in a long streamer, and stared down at a squad car moving out on some urgent errand, an errand for Gideon. "Goddam Mr. Bloody Commander Gideon!" he said explosively.

He knew Gideon as a kind of legendary father figure at the Yard, but had had very little to do with him. He knew that most C.I.D. men would go all the way with their Commander, and the Uniformed men felt much the same. There was talk that Gideon would one day be Assistant Commissioner for Crime as a stepping-stone to the Commissioner's job when Scott-Marle retired. This might be part of the plan for him.

It certainly wasn't part of his, Cox's, plans or hopes.

Cox was not able to see the situation objectively enough, at that moment, to know that he was angry because it was the first real slowing down in his career. At thirty-nine, he was by seven years the youngest Deputy Commander of the five at the Yard, and at thirty-nine he believed that he should have been in charge of his branch for this big job. Instead, he was passed over—in fact put aside—for Gideon.

"He doesn't know a thing about Uniform," Cox said in a hard whisper. The telephone bell rang. "You sure you don't want Gideon?" he growled, and then he gave a short, amused laugh at himself, strode over, and picked up the receiver. "Deputy Commander," he announced.

"Mr. Cox?" asked a man with a deep, penetrating voice.

"Yes."

"This is George Gideon," the latter said, and Cox thought: *Of course, this couldn't be anyone else's voice.* "Will you be in if I come over and see you in about twenty minutes?"

Cox paused.

Gideon began: "If it's a bad time—"

"No, it's as good a time as any," Cox said. "I will expect you, Commander."

"Right, then. I'll be there," said Gideon, and rang off.

3

THE OTHER SIDE OF THE LAW

WHEN the evening newspapers came out with their headlines :

WESTERN SUMMIT FOR LONDON
BIG FOUR MEET IN JUNE

and gave details already released by the Home Office about the procession route for the State Visits, some men's eyes sparkled at the thought of the illegal profit likely to come their way as a result.

One of these was a little, perky man named Alec Sonnley. He had bright green-grey eyes, a shiny little pink-and-red face, and was always smartly dressed. When the sun shone on him he looked rather like an apple half hidden by leaves, for he wore a green hat, and his clothes were always green, grey-green or browny-green. The most noticeable things about him, apart from his rosy, shiny complexion, were his hands and feet, which were much larger than average, making a man of five feet six look a little ridiculous.

Everyone called him Sonny Boy, partly because of his name, partly because of his habit of whistling popular songs—like an errand boy. Actually there was nothing at all boyish about Sonny Boy. He had carefully and very skilfully organized a business in London which had all the outward appearance of being legitimate. He ran a large wholesale warehouse in the Petticoat Lane district of the East End, from which he supplied street traders and hawkers, as well as small shopkeepers from the Greater London area.

In addition to this, he owned thirty shops, all in popular shopping areas, all dealing in what he called "*Fancy*

Goods, Jewellery, Gold and Silver Articles". In each shop he had a manageress and two or three assistants, and each member of the staff was strictly honest—none of them knew that he or she was dealing in stolen goods.

To make discovery much less likely, Alec Sonnley bought up a great deal of bankrupt stocks, salvaged goods, and low-priced ornaments, in all of which he did good business. No single item in any of his stores cost over five pounds, and he had a series of "special advertising offers" at five shillings and ten shillings each. At least half his stocks were stolen goods.

He also had the third aspect of the business worked out just as carefully as the retail and wholesale angles. He used six steady shop-lifters and eight steady handbag and pocket pickers, or snatchers and dips. This team operated in big shopping areas, especially in the West End of London or in the bigger surburban districts. These thieves concentrated on stealing branded goods, which were taken to the retail outlets and sold quickly.

Sonnley paid his pickpockets a retainer all the year round.

Every now and again, especially when he believed that the police suspected one of them, he "rested" these operatives, but because of the retainer they were ready to work again the moment he felt it safe.

The great simplicity of his system helped Sonnley to success. Quick-selling goods stolen from one part of London were often on sale in another part on the same day, for he had a plain van driven by his chief operative, a man named Benny Klein, who made the rounds regularly, collecting and delivering. Anything of real value, Sonnley disposed of through ordinary receivers.

No one knew quite how much he was worth, but it probably approached a quarter of a million pounds.

Any attraction which drew the crowds to the heart of London would set Sonny Boy whistling chirpily. His pickpockets, bag-snatchers and shop-lifters often quadrupled their takings, and his wholesale warehouse supplied hundreds of street traders with souvenirs.

That Tuesday, he drove from the small suite of offices in a narrow street near Baker Street Station, and out of the corner of his eye saw a newspaper placard : WESTERN SUMMIT FOR LONDON. He slowed down by the next news boy, and kept a dozen cars waiting behind him while he bought a newspaper. Very soon he began to whistle, and the whistle became gayer while he drove to St. John's Wood, where he had an apartment near Regent's Park. He turned into the underground garage, then whistled his way across to the lift which would take him up to the seventh floor, and his wife. He was married to a plump, good-natured woman with thin, metallic-looking reddish-yellow hair. She loved expensive clothes, loved her Sonny Boy and, rather unexpectedly, loved cooking. So Sonnley went home to lunch whenever he could.

His tune was rounded and full as he stepped out opposite his apartment, Number 71, and let himself in. There was a faint aroma of frying onions, which suggested a steak or mixed grill. When he went into the spotless tiled kitchen, the steaks were sizzling and the onions seemed to be clucking. Rosie glanced round, saw him, and immediately plunged a basket of newly sliced chips into a saucepan of boiling fat. A great hiss and a cloud of steam came.

Sonnley went across and slid his arm round his wife's comfortable bosom, squeezed, gave her neck a peck of a kiss, and said :

"I hope it's good. We've got a lot to celebrate."

"Oh, have we, Sonny dear?" said Rosie. "What is it?"

"Believe it or not, sweetie-pie, we're going to have a State Procession for a great big Western Four Power Summit meeting in li'l old London Town," declared Sonnley, and held the newspaper up.

Reading, Rosie looked more and more puzzled.

"I'm sure it will be very nice, dear. Can I have a seat?"

"A what?"

"There are bound to be some wonderful stands put up for the Procession. In the Mall, I shouldn't wonder, or perhaps near the Abbey. You know, where the Houses of Parliament are." Rosie prodded a steak. "It's a pity it isn't a wedding, really. I do love to see them coming out of the Abbey with their lovely dresses. There will be stands, won't there?"

"You can bet your life there will!"

"And can I have a seat?"

"Front row, dead centre, the best there is," Sonnley promised. "Rosie, that steak smells wonderful. How long will it be?"

"About ten minutes."

"Just time for me to make a phone call," said Sonnley. He went out in the hallway, rubbing his hands, turned into a big drawing-room which overlooked the park, beyond the gardens of the building. The drawing-room had been furnished by a large London store, and although Sonnley was never sure why, he realized that it was as nearly perfect as it could be. The colourings were wine-red and pale blue. The furniture was mid-nineteenth century French. He sat at the end of a long couch, dialled a Whitehall number, and was answered almost at once by a man with a slightly foreign accent.

"Benny, you seen the papers?" Sonnley asked.

"Sure, I've seen the papers," answered Benny Klein.

"You getting ready to throw your hat in the air?"

"I'm getting ready all right," said the man with the accent. "I thought I'd be hearing from you."

"Just have a word with all the boys and girls, and tell them to have a week or two off," said Sonnley. "I don't want anyone in trouble between now and you-know-when. All okay?"

"Holiday with pay, is it?"

"You've got it in one, Benny," Sonnley agreed. "And I've got a little vacation planned for you, too."

"*Me?* I'm going to the Riviera, Sonny Boy. You know that."

"Not now you're not," Sonnley declared. "Buy your lay a nice diamond bracelet, and tell her to stay home and be a good girl. You know what's going to happen, don't you?"

27

"I'm not going to alter my plans for anybody." Klein was suddenly harsh-voiced.

"Now take it easy, Benny, take it easy! No one said anything about altering your plans. It's just a little postponement, that's all. You can take the girl with you if she loves you so much! You're going up to Glasgow, Liverpool, Manchester and Birmingham, and you're going to tell the boys up there to keep out of the Big Smoke when the V.I.P.s are here. We don't want any of those provincials muscling in on our London, do we?" When Klein didn't answer, Sonnley repeated sharply. "Do we?"

Klein said gruffly: "No, we don't."

"And I don't know anyone who can tell them so better than Benny Klein," said Sonnley. "Just make them understand that they keep out. See? If they don't, they'll run into a lot of trouble. Can you make them understand, Benny?"

"They'll understand," Klein asserted in a stronger voice.

"That's more like it," Sonnley approved. "Tell them I'll organize every gang of razor and chain-boys in London if provincials come down here. And when you've warned them good and proper, Benny, you can come down here and talk to the London gangs."

After a pause, Klein said: "The London gangs will want some dough."

"They'll get it, don't you worry. The same terms as for Maggie's wedding—they'll be okay. And tell your lady friend you'll buy her a mink stole as well, if she gives you a good time in England and forgets all about the Contingong." Sonnley chuckled. "Okay, Benny?"

"I suppose so."

"I thought it would be," Sonnley said. "See you, boy."

He rang off, stood for a moment by the telephone, and frowned. He had far too much on Benny Klein for Benny to be rebellious, but if he should get awkward, it would make a lot of difficulties.

"But he won't get awkward," Sonnley reassured himself, and began to whistle, but on a slightly subdued note.

28

After a few minutes he joined Rosie, who had now laid the table. A steak which looked juicy and tender teased Sonnley from its silver dish. The chips were a golden brown, and there were peas and broad beans as well as deep-fried onion rings.

"What's the matter, Sonny? Doesn't it look nice?" inquired Rosie.

"Blimey, it looks as if it's sitting up and begging to be eaten! Don't worry about me, I was just thinking about a business acquaintance who might need a little watching. Now, let's go!"

Sitting in a small Chelsea café and tucking into a plate of bacon, sausages, eggs and chips, was Michael Lumati, well known to Alec Sonnley, and also well known to the police, although it was now three years since he had been under suspicion of any crime, and five since he had been in prison.

On that occasion he had earned full remission after a three-year sentence for issuing forged banknotes. According to his own story, he now earned a reasonable living by selling lightning portraits at fairs and race-courses, for ten shillings a time. He also designed calendars and programmes, and did a few catalogues—including Sonnley's.

Lumati had a small studio at the top of one of the old, condemned buildings of Chelsea, not far from the river, and he spent a lot of time in the studio, usually cooking his own breakfast and evening meal, but going out for lunch. Today he sat in a corner of the café, a man nearing fifty, rather thin, with a healthy looking, tanned complexion, very clear grey eyes, and a small Van Dyck beard. That, and the faded beret which he always wore at the back of his head, made him look the part of an artist.

Some of his craftsmanship, at its best in copies of currency notes, was unbelievably good. When he had been caught, experts had agreed that it was almost impossible to tell the difference between his work and the real thing.

He had a copy of the London *Standard* propped up against the wall at his side, and kept reading the story of the coming State Procession. There was a calculating expression in his eyes. The police did not know that, after years of experiment and error, Lumati had succeeded in drawing a line which looked as if it were a tiny thread through the paper—making detection nearly impossible—nor did the police know that he had tens of thousands of these one-pound and ten-shilling notes printed and ready for distribution.

He knew a man who would want plenty of paper money at the time of the visit, too. Sonny Boy Sonnley.

One other man, an almost pathetic, elderly clerk in a shipping office, earning only twelve pounds ten a week, was preparing to make hay in a very different way. Money itself did not greatly interest him. When he first read of the coming visit, his heart had leapt because of the fact that the next time the Head of the French Republic appeared in London he, Matthew Smith, was to act as assassin. He was by no means matter-of-fact about it, but was very sure of success. It had been planned so carefully.

The police and the security forces would be watching all the likely sources of danger in London, of course, and airports and railway terminals would be closely watched to make sure that no terrorists arrived there. Probably all possible suspects would be rounded up before the visit—but that would make no difference at all.

No one would suspect such a mild little Englishman as Matthew Smith of hating France so bitterly, or of having so much power in his hands.

Still less would they suspect that he also hated his wife, simply because she had always tried to soften his attitude towards the French, and so had drawn some of his venom upon herself.

At that time, however, the thought of murdering his wife had not crossed his mind. He exulted only because he would soon be the man—perhaps the martyr—who had killed the leader of France.

4

CONFLICT?

"Very good, Commander," Cox said formally.

"If we get started early it shouldn't be much trouble," Gideon said.

"No."

"I shouldn't think we'll need any U.B. men from the Provinces. Do you?" asked Gideon. He felt strangely uneasy. The interview with Cox hadn't gone right, largely because of Cox's stiffness—not really obstructiveness, but next-door to it. In a way he reminded Gideon of workers who would not come out on strike, but worked strictly to rule. He wished that he knew the man better, then he could judge whether Cox was simply resentful of the situation, or whether he was often like this. Instead of saying, "I shouldn't think we'll need any U.B. men from the Provinces," it would have been better to say: "Do you think we'll need any?"

"I have had no experience of a situation like this," Cox answered. "I can hardly advise."

The manner in which the words were uttered annoyed Gideon, and for the first time, he thought: *I'm going to have to watch him.* He stared into Cox's very bright dark blue eyes, and read the defiance in them. If he used the wrong tactics now he might make co-operation extremely difficult, and he had plenty to do without adding a kind of departmental feud.

So he ignored Cox's retort.

"Have a closer look at the figures of Uniform Branch men used for the Coronation," he said. "That's the guide the C.I.D.'s working on."

"Very well," said Cox.

"Give me a ring when you've checked, will you?" asked Gideon, and went out.

He was subdued as well as uneasy, not at all sure that he had been wise to ignore that retort; had it been one of his own men he would have reacted sharply. He simply didn't yet know how best to handle Cox, but already the dangers as well as the difficulties inherent in taking over another branch were threatenng.

Joe Bell was at his desk, coat off and collar and tie loose, because it was so warm. In a different mood Gideon might have asked Bell's opinion about Cox, but, in any case, Bell was obviously preoccupied.

"What have you got there?" Gideon demanded.

"Just running over that list of the chaps we ought to watch for the Visit," said Bell. "When are you going out to the Divisions?"

"I'll make a start next week," said Gideon. "I'll do a memo for them first, and warn 'em I'm coming. Heard anything from Lemaitre?"

"No."

"Write to him, and write to the Chief Constables of the big provincial cities—Glasgow, Manchester, Liverpool, Birmingham, Bristol, and any others where they might plan to send raiding parties to pick up as much loot as they can for the Visit. Ask for reports on all gangs, all pick-pockets, shop-lifters and con-men—you know, the usual. If any of them start planning a little holiday in London, we want to know."

"Right," said Bell.

"If you get the letters off today they'll have 'em in the morning. Tomorrow afternoon you can telephone the Superintendents and ask them to play."

"They'll play," said Bell, confidently.

"I hope you're right," said Gideon. "Now I've got to go along and have a cuppa with those Aussies. The A.C.'s putting on a bun fight for them." He went out, thinking about Cox, looking almost ponderous as he walked along the passages. He rounded the corner to Rogerson's office, and found a grey-haired sergeant on duty outside; some of the elderly men became little more than messengers in their last year or so of service. "Hallo, Charlie," said Gideon. "How's that ankle of yours?"

"Could be worse, Mr. Gideon, but it's been dry lately. In wet weather it's something cruel. You going in?"

"Think they'll let me?"

"Wouldn't be surprised," said the sergeant. He pushed the door open, and a babble of voices came from twenty men and two women—women whom Gideon hadn't expected, who had been tacked on to the Australian touring party.

The doorway between Miss Timson's office and the A.C.'s showed thick with tobacco smoke. In the smaller office a long table had been set with cups and saucers, sandwiches and cakes, and Gideon espied Miss Timson carrying two cups of tea to men standing a little on their own in a corner. They brightened up at sight of her. Not a bad-looking woman, Gideon thought, as another girl in the secretarial pool came with tea and sandwiches. He was swept into the talk, had a few minutes' chat with young Wall, sensed that everyone had enjoyed themselves, discovered that one of the women was an Australian newspaper reporter, and the other an American publisher of crime stories, who had come with an introduction from Police Headquarters in New York.

At a quarter past five the Australians went off. In the littered room, Miss Timson and some canteen helpers were busy packing dirty crockery on to trays. Rogerson was looking out of the window.

"Glad that's over?" asked Gideon.

"Very," said Rogerson. "It wasn't my day for making pretty speeches. Miss Timson, how soon can I have my office free?"

"In five minutes, sir."

Rogerson said. "Try and make it four. Is Bell in your room, George?"

"Yes."

"I've been like a bear with a sore head all day," said

Rogerson, under his breath. "Scott-Marle annoyed me by putting that lot on your shoulders. How did Cox take it?"

"He'll do."

"Hope you're right," said Rogerson. "Ripple's going to start his flying vacation on Friday, just as soon as he's got all the Algerian nationalists in London checked. He thinks that the Algerians are as likely a source of trouble as any. Some anti-American lunatic might take a pot at the President of the United States, of course, and the country's still full of people who think the Germans are all Nazis. No special reason to expect trouble, though, is there?"

"Shouldn't think so," Gideon said, but was more acutely conscious of a sense of disquiet, almost certainly due to Cox. He saw Miss Timson coming out of Rogerson's office, looking very prim.

"Your room is in order, sir."

"Thanks," grunted Rogerson. He and Gideon went into the office, and Miss Timson closed the door on them.

All trace of the invasion had gone. Ash-trays had been emptied, the windows were wide open, there was little odour of smoke, and the place had a new-pin look.

Rogerson said lugubriously: "She's so damned efficient it's almost a crime to grumble at her."

"Are you worried about the German Group?" Rogerson wanted to know, next morning. Obviously he had been preoccupied by this overnight.

"There's always the lunatic fringe of anti-Germans," Gideon said. "And the really bitter people who lost sons or—" he paused, as Rogerson looked at him steadily. "What I mean is, if anyone had a crack at the German President, it wouldn't necessarily be any organized group, more likely some individual, brooding by himself over some war-time grief. We caught three of them on the 1956 visit, remember?"

"Yes. Anyone in mind?"

"We can't have."

"Suppose not," conceded Rogerson.

34

Just before six o'clock the evening before, Gideon entered his office. He wasn't surprised to see Abbott standing by Joe Bell's desk. Abbott had that strong-man look about him, but was clenching his hands, as if keenly aware of tensions. His voice was a little too hearty.

"I hope I'm not too early, Commander."

"No, it's about right," said Gideon. "Did you get those letters off, Joe?"

"I'm just going along to the typing pool, to sign 'em for you," said Bell. "Anything else for me tonight?"

"No, thanks."

Bell went out, nodding good-night. Abbott was sitting on an upright chair, unable to relax. Gideon pushed his chair back against the wall, loosened his collar and tie again, and pushed cigarettes across the desk; when Abbott took one, his fingers were unsteady.

Gideon asked bluntly: "What's the trouble, Abb? Anything wrong anywhere?"

Abbott echoed: "Wrong?"

"I can't see Carraway worrying you as much as you're worried," said Gideon. "If we don't charge him now, we can later—it isn't a matter of life and death, is it?"

Abbott echoed: "Life and death." He drew deeply at the cigarette, and then said: "George, I'm in a hell of a spot. I really am. I ought to have brought Carraway in forty-eight hours ago. You remember I told you about the Belman girl? I've checked closely, and there isn't any doubt that Carraway spent the night of the murder with her. If he was with her, he wasn't playing cards with the men. So they lied."

"They might say they lied to save her reputation. We can work on them, but it looks like a switch from one alibi to a better one. That doesn't help us much."

"Don't I know it!" said Abbott. "Anyway, I questioned her yesterday morning, then put a couple of detective constables on to watching her—thought I might be able to wear her nerves down. Now she's disappeared. I can't help wondering if Carraway's got her. If she knows anything, she might crack under pressure, and—well, she's vanished."

Gideon said: "Carraway might have paid her to go away somewhere." He lifted a telephone which had a direct line to Information, and when a man answered he said: "Gideon here. I want a general call out, London, Home Counties, ports and airports, for a girl whom Superintendent Abbott will tell you all about. He'll be along in five minutes. Put a call out saying that this girl's wanted for questioning—what's her name, do you say?"

"Marjorie Belman."

"One L or two?"

"One."

"Marjorie Belman," Gideon repeated into the telephone, and added. "One L," before ringing off. "Let's get the full description, her address, everything you know about her." His tone belied the urgency of his actions, he knew that he would have to be very careful if he was not to drive Abbott into a nervous flap. "Can you give it to me straight?"

"Yes," said Abbott. He seemed clearer voiced and steadier, as if the vigour of Gideon's reaction had already done him good. "Marjorie Belman, aged twenty or so, height five-five or six, weight about eight stone, size 32, 27 or so, 36—"

"Flat chested?"

"Not big and busty anyway," Abbott said. "Nut brown hair, like a feather mop, dark blue eyes, slightly olive complexion, rosebud mouth . . ."

A picture of the girl etched itself on his mind as he talked.

5

THE FEARS OF MARJORIE BELMAN

BRUCE CARRAWAY had always been able to make Marjorie Belman do what he wanted.

She could never really recall what had happened on the first night they had met, but she remembered waking, naked body next to his naked body, and remembered the sense of shock and even of shame, until he had wakened, and looked at her through his dark lashes, and then caressed her, kissed her, possessed her. She would never forget the ecstasy, and yet she could never be wholly without shame. The awful moment had been when she had gone home after work next evening, and had a violent quarrel with her father when he had accused her of lying to him. The scene with her mother, who had begged her to tell the truth, had been nearly as bad. Only her elder sister, Beryl, had shown any understanding or sympathy.

She had left home for the tiny two-roomed flat, everything she needed paid for by Bruce. She had television, better clothes, a luxurious bathroom—and she did not need to work. Since then happiness and ecstasy had been her bedfellows, and apart from the shadow of the dismay of her parents, she had known nothing but contentment. Beryl had been to see her three times, and the last time had tried to make her go back home, but her first real anxiety had been over Arthur Rawson's murder.

Had Bruce killed him?

She wasn't really sure, only feared that he had—because she had heard him saying to Eric Little that "dear old Arthur would be better out of the way". She was to meet Bruce at six o'clock on the Swan & Edgar corner of Piccadilly, and already her heart was beating fast at the prospect—partly excitement, partly fear. She had to find out the truth about that murder, because the police kept on questioning her. They had, only that day. (It was the day when Abbott had talked to Gideon.)

Marjorie was ready to leave, and actually closing the door of her flat, when she heard footsteps downstairs, and then her older sister's voice. "Is Miss Belman in, do you know?" Beryl was talking to the liftman. Tight-lipped, Marjorie went forward, and Beryl caught sight of her.

"Jorrie!" she exclaimed.

"Beryl, it's no use talking, I'm not coming home," Marjorie said thinly. "I've told you before—"

"Jorrie, *please* listen to me," Beryl pleaded. She was slightly taller, had a fuller figure than Marjorie, and was quite as attractive. Now tension and desperation made her eyes shine. "I've simply got to make you understand that Mum's terribly ill. If you don't come back—"

The liftman was very near them.

"For heaven's sake, don't talk so loudly," Marjorie said angrily. "Everyone will hear you. Anyhow, I can't wait now."

"You've got to listen to me!" Beryl put a hand on her sister's arm. "If you don't leave that man, it will kill Mum. She's like a ghost walking, she's terrible. And Dad's nearly as bad."

"They'll get over it, like thousands of strait-laced parents before them," Marjorie said. "You're the real fool, for getting so worked up about it. If you can't mind your own business, I don't want to see you again, either."

"Jorrie, you don't know what you're doing."

Marjorie said thinly: "Let go of my arm, and if you can't be friendly, stay away from me." She wrenched herself free and half-ran out of the hallway into the street. The door swung to behind her.

Half-way along the street toward Piccadilly she glanced round, but there was no sign of Beryl. She was breathing heavily, still angry, but now partly with herself. Why had Beryl chosen such an awkward time? Why wouldn't she leave her alone? Parents were always the same anyhow—

why, her father had practically driven her away from home.

When she reached Piccadilly Circus, she watched every well-dressed man in the distance, longing to see Bruce. The bustle of traffic and of people was all around her. The pavements seemed hot, the petrol fumes smelly. A coloured couple came walking along, arm-in-arm, oblivious of the heart of London. Marjorie kept looking across at the tiny statue of Eros.

A middle-aged man sauntered up to her. "Would you care for a drink, my dear?" She glared at him. "Now come on—" the man began, and then broke off and moved away quickly. Marjorie saw a youthful-looking policeman staring at her; he had frightened the man off, but her heart began to pound. She was so scared of the police.

Why didn't Bruce come? She felt as if everyone was staring at her, saw a youngish man with a bushy moustache bearing down on her, with a beaming smile. She turned and walked away.

"Now, come, darling—"

It was beastly.

The policeman walked towards her and the man with the bushy black moustache marched past. She thought the policeman was going to speak, but he did not. She had no idea how pretty and lonely she looked, how many men glanced at her, almost wistfully.

She kept looking round for Beryl but did not see her; that was one good thing.

When at last she heard a familiar voice, it wasn't Bruce's.

"Waiting for someone, Jorrie?"

She turned quickly, to see Eric Little. He was short and stocky, his black hair was curly, and he had a very bright smile. He wouldn't have been so bad, except for the fact that whenever Bruce was out of the way, he was likely to slide his arm round her waist, or nuzzle her neck.

"I—I thought Bruce would be here by now," she said, acutely disappointed.

39

"He got held up," said Eric, "so he asked me to come and collect you. Had to go down to Brighton, you see. Be a nice night for the drive, won't it!" He put his hand on her arm and led her towards Piccadilly; his black Austin Cambridge was parked near the hotel. His grasp was firm, but with no hint of impudence of familiarity. She got into the car beside him. Soon, the cool evening air swept in through both windows, caressing her.

She had a final look round but saw no sign of Beryl.

Eric chose the Fulham and Putney Road, which was slightly longer but less busy. Marjorie noticed that he kept glancing at her, which puzzled her. Usually, even if she felt his fingers at her knees, she would look at him angrily, and find him staring straight ahead. This evening, he kept stabbing those strange glances at her. He drove very fast once they were on the open road, especially after turning off towards Guildford; as if he had something on his mind.

"Eric, why did Bruce have to go to Brighton tonight?" Marjorie asked suddenly.

"Big bizz, old girl."

"He didn't tell me about it."

"Can't tell the little lady everything."

"Eric—"

"Yes, sweetie?"

"Is everything all right?"

He looked at her sharply.

"What's that?"

"Is everything all right?"

"Why shouldn't it be?"

"I—I thought Bruce's been rather—rather worried lately."

"Old Bruce? Not on your life!"

After a few minutes' silence, she moistened her lips and said:

"Eric?"

"Yes?"

"It isn't any use lying to me."

"As if I would."

"Eric, Bruce is frightened of the police, I know he is. So am I. I—I'm afraid of what I'll say if that man comes again."

"What man?"

"The detective."

"That man Abbott you told Bruce about?"

"Yes."

"Forget him, honey bun."

"Don't be ridiculous," Marjorie said.

"Listen, Jorrie," said Eric in that rather high-pitched voice, "I tell you there's no need to worry. Bruce is fixing things. We're going to smuggle you out of the country." When Marjorie caught her breath, his left hand gripped her firmly just above the knee. "Bruce knows that it worries you when the police ask questions. He didn't have anything to do with the murder of his partner, it's only a matter of time before we prove it, but meanwhile—well, he doesn't want you worried by the police and he's fed up with them, too. He's on board a big motor yacht, off Brighton. You and Bruce are going to have a nice little holiday, going all the way to the Riviera. I'm going to take you out to the yacht as soon as it's dark."

Marjorie felt quite sure that Bruce was running away, and it scared her. But she loved him so, she *had* to be with him. And—the Riviera was wonderful.

They had dinner at Horsham, and night had fallen by the time they reached Brighton. Eric kept joking about a Riviera "honeymoon". She would not let herself think about the probability that Bruce was really running away. She could hardly wait to see him. A small motor-boat was waiting on the beach some distance from the main piers; the fact that it was a quiet spot didn't surprise Marjorie at all.

When they were some distance out to sea, with the lights of the two piers and the promenade like diamonds and emeralds, rubies and sapphires, reflecting on the calm water, she had a creepy feeling. She couldn't understand

41

why Bruce hadn't turned up by now. Why was Eric taking her so far in this small motor-boat? It was cold, too.

Eric moved away from the wheel.

"We'll let Oswald the automatic pilot take over," he said jocularly. "Listen, Jorrie—" He slid his arm round her. "Old Bruce won't be long . . ."

Soon she felt the boat slowing down, and realized that Eric had cut out the engine; they were going round and round in circles. She tried to push Eric away, but he was too strong for her. Suddenly fear came over her like a great wave. He was holding her in a peculiar way; he was lifting her from her seat, he—

She realized suddenly what he was going to do, and with a surge of terror, she kicked and struck out at him. But he just swung her over the edge of the boat, and dropped her into the sea. She tried to scream, made a funny gurgling sound, and took in a mouthful of water. It made her retch and choke. She struggled wildly to reach the surface, but as she did so a weight pressed against her shoulders.

She felt a sharp pain, on her right shoulder, as her head went under.

Eric was kneeling on the edge of the boat, pressing her down, down, down.

Undressing Marjorie when she was dead made Little feel sick. Dragging on the bikini pants, tying the bikini top about her little soft breasts, was horrible. Pushing her body into the sea again was a relief. He started the engine almost at once, and the pale blur that had been Marjorie Belman sank slowly out of sight.

Now all he had to do was to get rid of her clothes.

Beryl Belman got off the bus at the end of Carmody Street, Clapham, and walked quickly towards her home, Number 43. The long street had three-storey houses of red brick on either side, and each house looked very like the next. A few people were walking along, a motorcyclist passed, a woman from next-door-but-one came hurrying, stopped, and said :

"Beryl, dear, I do hope your mother's feeling better. She's been looking so ill lately."

"She's a bit run down," Beryl said, and thought : *The nosey old bitch, she knows what's happened.* "I must hurry, Mrs. Lee."

Actually, she did not want to hurry, for she hated what she would find. She squared her shoulders, put on a bright smile, and knocked at the front door. Her father opened it, looked at her searchingly, and then half-closed his eyes as if he knew she had failed. As she went in, he said :

"So you didn't see her."

"Yes, I saw her," Beryl said. "She wouldn't listen, that's all." Suddenly all her courage died away, and tears stung her eyes. "It's no use, Dad. It's no use at all."

"Don't tell your mother you saw her," her father ordered. He was a short, thin, harassed-looking man. His lack of a son had always hurt him, and too often driven him to outbursts of spiteful bad temper. Now, Beryl knew, he reproached himself dreadfully because he was partly responsible for driving Jorrie away. "Don't tell her, Bee. She's—she's a little bit better, I think. Don't tell her, just say that Jorrie was out."

From the kitchen along the hall, his wife called :

"Is that Beryl ?"

"Yes, Mum !"

"Well, don't stand there whispering to your father. Have you seen Jorrie ?"

Beryl lied : "No, Mum. She wasn't in."

Her mother stared at her as if with doubt and suspicion. Eyes which for so long had been gentle with love for her daughters, and pride in their appearance, were lack-lustre, red-rimmed, far too prominent. A soft voice had become harsh, a mild manner had become impatient and sharp.

"Don't lie to me, Beryl !"

"But, Mum, I—"

"It's bad enough to have a daughter go off and live in

43

sin, without having another who lies to me. Did you see Jorrie?"

Slowly, helplessly, Beryl said. "Yes."

"And she won't come home?"

"She—she won't yet, Mum. She—"

"She won't ever come home, I know that," said Mrs. Belman, in a strangled voice. "I've lost her. I've lost my Jorrie. I've lost . . ."

Quite suddenly, she crumpled up. As she fell, Belman pushed past Beryl, thrust her mother towards a chair and saved her from falling heavily, then stood looking down at her ashen face and at her slack mouth. Watching them, twenty-two-year-old Beryl Belman dedicated herself to a task which she did not dream was impossible of achievement.

"I'll make her come home," she pledged silently. "I'll make her realize what Carraway really is, and what she's done."

It was easy enough to tell her parents, after supper, that she was going out to a dance club. At half past eight she walked briskly and determinedly along the street, caught a bus at the end of the road, and went straight to Piccadilly. It was dark, but the lights flashed in a dozen colours, the Circus and the streets leading off were thronged. She saw a young constable stare at her, ignored him, and walked quickly, angrily, towards Alden Street, where Jorrie had her flat. The street door was open, and a small lift was at the end of a narrow passage. A light showed at the door of the caretaker's room, down in the sub-basement, but no one opened the door. Now her heart began to thump, for Marjorie was probably here, with Carraway. Even if they were together, she had to talk to Marjorie, and she could tell Carraway to his face what she thought of him.

The man must have *some* decency.

Beryl pressed the fifth and top floor button of the lift, stepped out, and stood in front of Marjorie's door. A light was on inside, so she was in. Beryl clenched her hands,

44

and her teeth, feeling a tension greater than ever she had known.

She *had* to talk to Jorrie, whether Carraway was there or not.

She pressed the bell, heard it ring, and stood back a pace, her teeth still clenched, words churning over and over in her mind : she must shock Jorrie into listening, had to make her pay attention.

Jorrie did not answer.

Tension and anxiety and a kind of fear began to melt together into anger. Carraway was in there with her sister, of course. They were probably in bed together. The last thing they would want was an interruption! Beryl stabbed at the bell again; nothing would make her go away until she had talked to Jorrie.

There was no answer.

"Jorrie!" she called out in a sharp voice. "I know you're in there. Come and open the door."

There was only silence.

Beryl put her finger on the bell-push, pressed hard, and kept it there, hearing the long, harsh, ringing sound. Surely no one could fail to answer it. It must be getting on their nerves.

"If you don't answer I'll go for the police!" she cried.

It was a threat drawn out of her by desperation, the only threat she could now imagine which might make Jorrie open the door. When the last word quivered on the stuffy air of the tiny landing, she felt that she had tried everything she knew, and lost. Tears of mortification and disappointment filled her eyes, and she turned away, not knowing what to do. The lift gates were open, behind her; and by the side of the lift was a narrow staircase. She stepped forward, and then heard a click of sound behind her. Her heart leapt. *Jorrie!* She spun round. The door of the flat was opening, but no light was on there. Only the light here showed that it wasn't Jorrie, it was a man.

He flung himself at her.

A cloth was pulled over his face and she could only just

45

see his eyes, dark, bright, glittering. She uttered a scream, but he struck her across the face, sending her reeling against the wall, silencing her. She slipped on the top step, and fell, banging her head painfully. Terror as great as her sister's welled up in her.

Then she heard a voice from below, loud and clear :

"What's going on up there?"

She heard other sounds, including a whining, and realized that the lift was going down. Through the iron trellis-work of the shaft she saw the man who had attacked her. The cloth had been pulled to one side, and she caught a glimpse of his profile before he disappeared below the level of the floor. The man from below called again :

"What's going on?"

Panic-stricken, she realized that she mustn't cause a scandal, for her mother would never stand it. She was dazed, frightened, unsure of herself, unable to grasp what had happened—but she must not cause a scandal. It would kill her mother, and Jorrie would never forgive her.

Beryl got up, slowly, awkwardly, and called : "It's all right, I slipped." She leaned against the wall, listening to the whine of the lift, hoping that the man on the floor below would not come up to investigate. She listened for the sound of footsteps, and believed that she heard him coming. She swayed away from the wall, and noticed that the door of Jorrie's apartment was open. She stepped inside quickly, and closed the door; it slammed. She stood in the darkness, heart thumping, eyes strained as they tried to accustom themselves to gloom broken only by a glow of light at the door.

No one called out.

At last, Beryl groped for the light switch, and found it. Blinking against the bright light, she went into the flat, with its furniture which to her seemed luxurious. Light in the big living-room came from a lamp with a monster shade. The television stared with square, vacant eye. Thick carpet cushioned her feet.

The bathroom, jade green in colour, made her gasp.

46

Everything here seemed all right, but Jorrie wasn't here; at least she hadn't refused to open the door.

But who had the man been? Who would come here alone by night, if it wasn't Carraway? And why should a man behave like that unless he was frightened?

Soon, Beryl went out, and down in the lift, and back home by bus. The next step, she told herself, was to find out where Carraway lived, and go and see him.

Bruce Carraway was not thinking about Marjorie or about Eric Little just then. He was busy making telephone calls in quick succession to private hire car dealers in the Home Counties, on the perimeter of London. He was obtaining options on cars and drivers at normal rates for the week of the Visit. Rental cars would be in great demand, whatever the weather.

In between calls, his telephone bell rang.

He hesitated, wondering who it was. Eric Little had already reported that the job at Brighton had been finished, so it wouldn't be Eric. It might be the police. Carraway lifted the receiver and said briskly:

"Bruce Carraway speaking."

"Bruce." It was Little again, and something in the way his name was uttered warned Carraway of trouble. "Bruce, I—I went round to—to her flat to get her things." There was a long, alarming pause. "I—I went to make it look as if she'd moved, like you told me, and—" Little was breathing very hard, and Carraway gripped the receiver tightly, but he did not speak. "Her sister called. She—she threatened to go to the police if the door wasn't opened. I got away all right, she didn't see me, but I had to leave the clothes and everything there."

Carraway said softly, slowly: "Keep away from that place until we know which way the police are going to jump. And keep away from me, except at the showrooms. Understand?"

Before Little had a chance to answer, Carraway rang off. He sat there, scowling, and it was a long time before he made his next call. Even then, he wasn't concentrating on business, but on this new danger. Supposing this sister had seen Little, after all? Supposing she could idéntify him?

That could make the difference between being safe, and being caught for a murder.

6

RIPPLE

AFTER the general call had gone out for Marjorie Belman, earlier that evening, Gideon studied Abbott's reports, and listened to everything the man said to amplify them. He could understand what had driven Abbott to make his decisions, and there was nothing in the preparation or the carrying out of the investigations which Gideon could fault. Abbott was sitting opposite him, still tense.

Gideon pushed the reports aside, bent down, opened a drawer in his desk, and took out a bottle of Scotch, two glasses, and a syphon.

"Like a nip?"

"Be glad of one."

"Say when," said Gideon, and in fact mixed Abbott's fairly strong, his own half-and-half. He pushed it across the desk, put his own glass to his lips, and said: "Here's to the end of crime," and sipped. He wouldn't have had a whisky, then, but for the need to give Abbott one. "Now," he went on, "if you'd come in yesterday morning and told me about the girl Belman, I would almost certainly have advised you to leave Carraway for a few days, and concentrate on the girl. I would also have told you to have her followed, and added the usual 'don't lose her'."

Abbott's eyes were brightening.

"You're not just saying this, George?"

"No," Gideon assured him. "I don't know how the case will work out, but I hardly think Carraway will kill the girl—he must know that it would be asking for trouble. Can't be sure, of course, but apart from that risk, there's only one thing I don't like."

Abbott went taut. "What's that?"

49

"The fact that you've dithered," Gideon said. He had a strange feeling, one which came every now and again and which he never liked but which had to be accepted for what it was. He was the headmaster, Abbott was the pupil in trouble; the relationship between two grown men was temporarily suspended. "Nothing wrong in the handling of the case, but there will be in future ones if you have the same approach. When did you last have a holiday with your wife?"

"Last year, but—" Abbott hesitated.

"Yes?"

"Well, we didn't go away," said Abbott. "Haven't been away for four years, as a matter of fact. Just messed around the house, going out for odd days. We have a bit of a problem at home."

Gideon thought: *Why didn't I know? Is this wife trouble?* "Sorry about that," he said. "Serious?"

"In itself it's not," replied Abbott, hesitantly. "It gets on my nerves, though. The wife's, too. We've got her mother living with us. The old soul's practically bedridden, and there's no one else to take over. Ties my wife all the time, and I can't very well go off on a holiday without her."

Normally Gideon would have told Abbott to fix a holiday of some kind, soon, and taken him off the job whether he liked it or not. But it simply couldn't be done. Every man on the Force would be needed until after the Visit.

"No sisters, brothers or relatives to take over for a week or so?" he asked.

"No one who will, George. You know how it is. My wife's always been the Martha in her family, and—" Abbott broke off.

"As soon as the V.I.P.s have gone home, you've got to take a few weeks off," Gideon compromised. "That's an order."

"Oh, sure," said Abbott.

After Abbott had gone, Gideon sat back, frowning. He had the frustrated feeling which often came to him, because he could not go out and tackle this job himself; that

50

feeling would probably come frequently in the next few weeks. But it was no use sitting and brooding. He did up his collar, tightened the knot of his tie, jumped up, and went out. He put his head round the corner of the office where the night duty Inspector was, said : "Nothing much to worry about, Mac, except this Marjorie Belman job. Seen that call?"

"Yep."

"Watch it. And in your spare time, check all duty rosters, holidays and special leaves, will you? Get as many holidays over as you can, before May 23rd, and postpone all of 'em after that a while, June 4th or 5th, say."

"Big Visit blues," the other man said. "Okay."

Gideon strode on, nodding good-nights right and left, until he reached the courtyard and saw someone standing by the side of his car, back from its check-up. When he drew nearer, he recognized Ripple. He frowned because he hadn't recognized the other at once. Usually his long sight was fairly good; he needed glasses only for continuous close work.

"Hallo, Rip."

"Going to be busy tonight, George?"

"Not specially," Gideon said.

"Think Kate will want to throw me out if I come round for an hour?"

"Come and have a meal with us," invited Gideon.

"Can't do that—I've a lot of odds and ends to clear up before I pack it in for tonight. I'll have a snack at the canteen. Okay if I come round about nine?"

"We'll have a drink anyhow."

"Good man," said Ripple.

There was something curiously secretive about him. In appearance he was much too heavy, almost coarse, and his face was badly pitted, probably from severe chicken pox as a child, although he had never said anything about it. He looked both tough and rough, but his voice was gentle, and whenever he was pleased he could not repress high spirits; whenever preoccupied, he seemed to brood.

Gideon reached Parliament Square, saw many more

cars there than usual at seven o'clock in the evening, then noticed that a car was on its side, blocking part of the road to Victoria Street. How could any driver manage to do that with a car on a perfectly dry road in a thirty miles an hour limit area in broad daylight? A constable came up.

"I'd filter through to the right if I were you, sir, and go through St. James's Park. Nasty business over there."

"How nasty?"

"Two stone dead, I'd say—pedestrians. And the driver of the car's a hell of a mess. He side-swiped a lorry—oh, there's the ambulance. Shall I see you through, sir?"

"Please," said Gideon. "Thanks." The constable moved on a dozen pedestrians from the middle of the square, and Gideon crawled past them. He saw a middle-aged woman being led away from the scene by a man; the woman looked greenish-yellow, as if she would be sick. As Gideon passed, she muttered : "Terrible, terrible."

He moved along with a line of traffic into St. James's Park, thinking of Cox, because Cox was in charge of Uniform except over the Visit, and accidents like these were handled by his Department. It was a hell of a job. For the first time, Gideon found himself wondering whether Cox was the right man to take the brunt of public and newspaper criticism about motoring and motorists. Whenever there was a big traffic jam the police were always blamed; the Visit would cause some of the biggest jams ever.

Gideon was half-way along Birdcage Walk when he caught sight of a man and a woman strolling along on the far side of the road, arm-in-arm. The woman was tall, had a nice figure and slim legs, and kept her shoulders straight. As he drew level he saw that it was Miss Timson —and, good God! Young Wall from Sydney. Thirty-five-year-old man and forty-five-year-old woman, if Gideon was any judge. The coincidence made him forget both the accident and Cox.

It was half past seven when he put the car into his garage round the corner from his house in Harrington

Street, Fulham, and locked the shutters and strolled round to the house. It hadn't been painted on the outside for three years, and ought to have a coat this year. Three or four years ago he would have taken that in his stride; it would be three week-ends' work at the most, if he could get three off duty in a row. He could forget that this summer—after the Visit he would be so involved with a backlog of normal work that week-ends off would be skimpy, to say the least.

He opened the iron gate, passed the neatly trimmed privet hedge and the trim, postage-stamp sized lawn, and as he did so, the door opened and his wife appeared.

"Hallo, dear! I was in the bedroom. I thought I saw the car pass."

She had been making-up for him; not too heavily, just enough to look fresh and appealing. She made up more these days than she had when she was young. She was tall, in fact a big woman, deep-breasted but with a well-defined waist, nice legs, rather large feet, narrow enough for shoes of fashion. Her hair was a lighter grey than Gideon's, and she'd had a set today. It was good to see the way her face lit up, good to feel the satisfaction which he felt; yet their kiss was light and almost casual.

"You look as if you're expecting visitors," Gideon said.

She looked pleased. "According to the news, you're expecting the visitors."

Gideon laughed, then told her all that had happened. Kate was quiet and thoughtful until they were sitting at the table. Gideon had a huge plate of meat pie in front of him, knife and fork at the ready. "Isn't it going to be rather a lot?" Kate asked.

"What?"

"Your ordinary job, *and* Uniform."

"It'll break my back!"

Kate gave a little laugh, and started to eat; five minutes later, she looked across at his empty plate, shook her head, and said:

"I suppose it's no use saying you'll ruin your digestion. You haven't improved in thirty years. George."

"Hm-hm?" Gideon was helping himself to more pie.

"Do you think you could get me a seat on the balcony of the Ministry?"

"Wouldn't be surprised," said Gideon. "I'll put in the request tomorrow."

He helped Kate to wash up, and at half past eight switched on the television. There was a news telecast at 8.45 to make time for a two-hour Shakespeare performance. Kate took out some of their son Malcolm's socks, drew them over her hand, found a small hole in one heel, and began to darn.

The news announcer reported the forthcoming Western Summit as if it were fresh and epoch-making. There were a few Russian comments, some African news, some home oddments, and finally:

"In reply to questions in the House of Commons today following his speech about the reduction in overall crime figures the Home Secretary said he fully realized that the improvement might be short term, and the police would certainly not relax their efforts in any degree. His speech was not intended to suggest that there were any grounds for complacency. In reply to Mr. Lubbock, Labour, West Ferry, he said that the improvement was certainly due to improved police methods in which scientific aids to the investigation of crime were being used to the full. There had been no material increase in police manpower. In reply to Mr. Ventry, Conservative, Lushden, he said that some measure of the improvement was undoubtedly due to the spell of severe cold weather in the month of March but he did not believe that this was a major cause. The major cause was undoubtedly the unceasing vigilance of the police, and the use of new methods of crime detection. In reply to Mr. Goss, Liberal, Ockney, he said that it was Government policy to put as much emphasis as possible on the prevention as distinct from the detection of crime, and that in the long run this would undoubtedly be the deciding factor. The Home Secretary added that he did not think that a long-term policy of

54

crime prevention would really enable anyone to sleep more easily in his bed tonight or for many nights to come —detective work by the Criminal Investigation Department and patrolling by the uniformed policemen were still the main weapons used against modern crime."

The announcer turned to some racing news.

"The Home Secretary sounds almost as if he's got some sense, doesn't he?" remarked Kate.

"Scott-Marle had a go at him," said Gideon. "We had a conference this morning . . ." He was half-way through a recital of what had happened at the conference when the front door bell rang. "That'll be Rip," he said. "I'll go." He had a queer little thought as he went to open the door. He wished this was Cox, come to discuss their joint problem, instead of Ripple.

Mildred Cox knew that Ray was in a gloomy mood almost as soon as he got home, just before seven o'clock. He was sharp with Tom, their only child, nine years old, whom he usually spoiled. Mildred's problem was to prevent a scene with the nine-year-old without making her intervention too obvious.

Everything she did to help Ray had to be unostentatious. Outwardly, he was the hub of the little family, and Mildred cheerfully went along with that. For one thing, she was so small and he so tall and rangy; seen from behind, they looked like father and daughter, for the top of her blonde head barely came up to his angular shoulders. She wore her soft, golden-blonde hair in a feather-like cluster. Her grey eyes were big and round with an expression of constant wonder. She had a button of a nose, and, like Ray, nice full lips and a little pointed chin.

Tom took after her in features and colouring, and promised to take after his father in height.

"Now you go along to your room and get your home-work done," Cox ordered his son. 'Don't let's hear another squeak out of you until it's finished."

"Okay, Dad."

"And don't say 'okay'. Use the English language."

"All right, Dad." Tom was always subdued when his father picked on him.

The boy went out of the long, narrow living-room, and closed the door quietly. In the corner, the 21-inch television screen was blank. This was a four-roomed apartment in Lambeth, just across the river from the Yard, in a square, squat new apartment building. The window overlooked the Thames, the Embankment, the training ships moored alongside, the passenger jetties, the Thames side jetty and the launches, the Victorian buildings cheek-by-jowl with modern blocks—and New Scotland Yard.

That was why they had moved here, five years ago.

When the boy had gone, Cox stood staring out of the window. A few lights were on, although there was another hour of daylight. The river was calm and beautiful. Boats skimming along it looked almost unreal. Cox kept looking at the C.I.D. block, grey and fairly modern; he could see Gideon's office window.

Suddenly, he said aloud: "We'll have to watch the river. Be a hell of a lot of extra traffic on it."

"When, dear?" asked Mildred, although she knew very well.

"During the next State Visit. Haven't you heard about it?"

"There *was* something on the television."

"It's going to be a very big show."

"I suppose so, with all those Presidents. There's one good thing, it won't interfere with our holiday this time, as we're not going until August. Will it mean a lot of extra work for you?"

"Not as much as it should."

"What a funny thing to say," murmured Mildred. She put down some of Tom's stockings, and smiled up. "You don't *want* more work, do you?"

"I wanted this," growled Cox.

"I think I must be extra dumb tonight," said Mildred, apologetically. "I don't know what you mean."

"Well, it doesn't take much explaining. I've been given

56

a kick in the pants, and . . ." He talked slowly at first, and then with increasing vigour, so that both bitterness and injured pride showed all too clearly. He walked about the room as he told her how Gideon had actually come to see him, to lay down the law and show his authority. By the time he had finished, it was nearly eight o'clock. More lights were on across the river, and a pleasure craft with festoons of coloured bulbs went swinging down-water.

"I think it's shameful," Mildred said hotly.

"Shameful's *one* word !"

"I always thought Commander Gideon was a good sort."

"There can be a big difference between a man and his reputation," Cox said sourly.

"I suppose there can," said Mildred, as if that was a new and profound reflection. After a pause, while she looked up at her husband's face, she went on : "I know what I would do."

"Do you?" asked Cox. When his wife made a pronouncement like that he was always mildly amused. Talking had helped a great deal, already, although he did not realize it. "And what would Mildred the miracle-worker do?"

"I'd do the job so well that it would teach Gideon a thing or two," declared Mildred. "I'd make sure I didn't put a foot wrong. *I'd* show them !"

Cox actually laughed. . . .

He was more his usual self with Tom, after homework and before bed ; and after Mildred had gone to bed he sat at a desk, outlining his plans for the Visit.

Mildred had something there, all right. He'd show Gideon.

Ripple stayed at Gideon's place until after midnight, long after Kate had gone to bed.

His chief worry was the tight time schedule. He knew that Gideon had plenty on his shoulders, and his own chief *aide* would be right on top of the job—but would he,

Gideon, keep an eye on anything which developed in the next week or ten days, especially in the next two or three days? If there were an influx of Algerians, for instance, they ought to be watched closely, and there was always the risk that they would work through some other groups.

"They might send a group of Algerian colonists over to distract us, and use someone we least expect to make an attempt on the French President," Ripple said. "Don't know why it is, George, but I've got a nasty feeling about this show. There isn't enough time to prepare properly. Can't very well tell Rogerson this, certainly not the Commissioner, but I thought you ought to know."

"Thanks," said Gideon. "I appreciate it." When he saw that Ripple had said all he wanted to say, he chatted idly for a few minutes, then went on: "What do you think of our Timson?"

"Vi?"

"That her name? I didn't think she was human enough to have one," Gideon said, with laboured humour.

"If you ask me," said Ripple, "Vi Timson's a bit of a dark horse. Why?"

"Just wondered," said Gideon, and had a mental picture of "Vi" walking along with the Australian detective inspector, at least ten years her junior. He added, as if casually: "Didn't you work at JK Division with Cox once?"

"Ray Cox?"

"Yes."

"Touched him on the raw, has it?" Ripple inquired shrewdly.

"Oh, I wouldn't say that. I just want to make sure it doesn't."

"Ray's all right," pronounced Ripple, judicially, "but he's gone ahead too fast. He ought to have had another two years on the beat, way back. Just the man I'd like beside me in a big job, though, provided I didn't rub him up the wrong way."

"So working with him should be easy—is that it?"

"Could be," corrected Ripple. "You'll either have to slap him down, or give him his head."

Ripple was often over-confident, whereas Abbott was not confident enough. Gideon thought a lot about Abbott —more, ironically enough, than he did of the Belman girl, or of Carraway.

7

THE BOMB

"Don't look now," said Ricky Wall, "but when you get a chance, tell me what you think of the man dancing with the blonde with the Edwardian hair style. He's like a big-time criminal who was murdered in Australia two years ago. We never caught the killer."

"I thought the Sydney police were *so* much better than ours."

"Cut that out," said Wall, with a grin. "Those boys at the Yard really know their job. You could try your well-known charm to find out what they think of the Australian party."

"Sometimes what I would like to use on the Yard men is *not* my well-known charm," said Violet. "Oh, they're so *smug*!"

"None of them pinched your bottom yet?" demanded Wall. "Vi, you're my girl. How about getting shot of this place, and seeing how well we can get to know each other between now and eight o'clock in the morning?"

"I have to be at the office at nine o'clock, so I've got to be up by half past seven," said Violet. "I'll think about your kind offer at the week-end."

Wall complained: "And I thought I was on a safe bet."

"Nothing about me is safe," said Violet, looking at him through her lashes. She wore a cocktail dress, high at the neck, but her arms were bare; she might be nearer fifty than forty, but she looked in the late thirties, and her skin was smooth and without blemish. "When does your party go back, Ricky?"

"We leave London on Tuesday, go over to Paris for three days, Berlin for three days, spend a week in Scandinavia, three days in Milan and another two in Rome, and then fly back here for a final few days in London. Just in time for the big Visit," he went on, and his eyes kindled. "I've always wanted to see what London puts on for these occasions."

"Where would you rather be posted—at the Palace, or at the Houses of Parliament?" asked Violet.

"Which do you recommend?"

"For a Colonial," said Violet, wickedly, "I would think the Palace."

"We hicks from the Dominions are great royalists but we are also true democrats," retorted Wall solemnly. "I'll be at the Houses of Parliament. Can you fix it?"

"Yes," said Violet, simply.

They went up the narrow stairs to the street, a turning off Bond Street. It was quite chilly. The doorman asked: "Cab, sir?" "No, thanks," said Wall. He slid his arm round Violet's waist, and raised his hand to cup her breast. "Change your mind," he pleaded.

She closed her hand over his.

"We'll have a wonderful week-end," she said. "But I have a lot to do in the morning, and I won't be in bed until nearly two o'clock as it is."

"Now who takes work to bed?" demanded Wall, but he laughed, squeezed, and lowered his hand. "I want you to know something," he said. "I think you're quite a girl." After a moment, he went on: "Do we need a cab?"

"It's only five minutes' walk," said the Assistant Commissioner's new secretary.

They walked, slowly.

Without knowing it, they passed the house where there was a small, empty flat, with Marjorie Belman's clothes still hanging in the wardrobe, her make-up things still on the dressing-table, food intended for that day still in the refrigerator.

Wall saw Violet to the front door of her flatlet in South Audley Street, and then strolled towards Piccadilly, smiling, half dissatisfied, half pleased with himself. He hailed a cab, gave his hotel address, and sat back.

As he got out of the taxi and glanced across the Thames, which he could hear lapping gently against the embankment, momentarily he looked straight in the direction of the little house in Streatham, not far from the common, where Matthew Smith was lying next to his wife in the big double bed, thinking of his bomb.

Smith was restless and on edge that night, filled with repressed excitement and impatience. He kept his thin, bony body as still as he could, for he believed his wife was asleep. She stirred unexpectedly and asked in a clear voice :

"Can't you sleep, dear ?"

So she was restless, too—almost as if she sensed his excitement and his tension.

"I'm all right," Smith answered gruffly.

"But I honestly don't think you are," his wife said. "You looked peaky all the evening. Matt, dear, what is it ? If I don't know, I can't help, can I ?"

He felt like striking her fat face, felt like shouting : "I tell you it's nothing !" Instead, he kept silent.

"Matt, is—is it because of the French—the Frenchman coming ? If it is, you mustn't let it upset you. It's so long ago, now, it—"

"I don't want to talk about it," he said in a hard voice. "If you can't go to sleep, keep quiet."

He woke early on Saturday morning, in spite of the bad night. He did not go to the office on Saturdays, and usually spent the morning in the small garden, with some fuchsias, his favourite flowers, or weeding the small herbaceous border, or pottering in his little workshop at the end of the garden.

In this workshop he had a carpenter's bench, a good selection of tools in two wall racks, and always some repairs waiting to be done. It was surprising how skilful he was with his thin, bony hands—which looked almost too frail to hold tools firmly. He was a good carpenter, and could French polish as well as most professionals. Any work with wood soothed him. All the furniture in the house was in perfect condition; as a handyman, no one could be more efficient. His married daughter often called upon him to do odd jobs.

It was a long, long time since his son had died—the eager-eyed, fresh-faced lad of nineteen who had gone out to France so happily for a three-months' training course in Grasse, the French perfume centre in the mountains behind the Riviera. His son—he always thought of the lad as "my son", hardly ever as Robert—had been keen on chemistry, and had got a job in the research department of a firm of cosmetic manufacturers on the Great West Road. His future had seemed very bright, and would have been but for the awful thing which had followed.

A girl had been murdered, and the French police had accused the boy.

Even today, twenty-five years afterwards, at the thought of the trial, at the thought of that awful slicing smash of the guillotine, Smith would feel his blood going hot and his hands clenching and unclenching, and sometimes he would break out into cold sweat. Ever since that awful day, Smith had hated France and the French with unreasoning, venomous hatred. Whenever the French were in trouble, Smith was elated; the political crises, the economic crises, the damaging strikes, the Algerian revolts— all of these were simply a vengeful fate. Years ago, when France had collapsed under the Panzer divisions and the Stukas, he had screamed aloud that the English were fools for ever trusting Frenchmen. He hated, hated, hated them.

His wife knew this.

From the beginning, she had tried to soothe him, saying that it wasn't just the French, it was the law everywhere. Anyone could make mistakes, and this had been an awful one; that was the way to look at it.

Smith had soon learned that she had no hatred in her heart for the French murderers, and that had been the beginning of his antipathy towards her, a slowly increasingly, deepening, bitter dislike.

Only when driven by physical need, did he touch her. Sometimes he wished her dead. He did not fully realize that his hatred had swollen to hideous size and shape.

One day a dark-skinned Frenchman had got into conversation with him on a bus, and started to damn his own country folk as colonialist aggressors, sadistic brutes, decadent morons in sex and art. Before long, Smith had been talking more freely to the dark-skinned man than to anyone he knew. All his hatred for France and the French had come out.

The man had asked if he would do anything to help the Algerian Colonists' cause. In his work as a shipping clerk Smith handled bills of lading, invoices, all kinds of things to do with imports and exports, and he often went on board ships in London docks, with these papers. Would Smith act as a messenger? the man asked. Sometimes it was useful to pass small packages, letters and secret information—it would be invaluable to the nationalist cause if Mr. Smith would help. And of course he would be paid for taking risks.

It wasn't very much money; just five pounds a week, every week. But it increased Smith's income by nearly a half. He told his wife that he had been given a rise, with a more important job, and as far as he knew, she believed it.

It was three years since the suggestion that he should take another, this time drastic, step; that of assassinating General de Gaulle on a state visit in 1960. For:

". . . no one in Algeria believes that he wants to end the war and make peace . . . His spies are everywhere . . . He will cheat us, like all the other leaders . . . See what happened to the real friends of the Nationalists . . . See how slow he is in redeeming his promises . . . We must shock the French nation and strike a great blow for the freedom of Algeria."

Matthew Smith had grown into the acceptance of the fact that this was exactly what he should do. It would be the ultimate act of vengeance for his dead son.

". . . and the best way is to throw a bomb, which we will provide for you. In London it is easy for you to be at the front of a crowd during a procession, and you can be within a few metres of the carriage in which de Gaulle will ride."

Smith went along to his workshop, on that Saturday morning, remembering that the great chance had been lost in 1959. Everything had been ready, the bomb had been in his possession, he had known exactly where he was to stand, and a few white sympathizers with the Algerian nationalist cause had been primed to help him to get away, by causing confusion in the ranks. Then on the day before the great opportunity he had woken with a terrible headache, aches and pains all over, and a matter-of-fact wife had called the doctor. His temperature had been a hundred and four. He had not even been able to stagger across the room. Luckily, he had been able to satisfy the others that it had not been last-minute fright.

He had never really recovered from the disappointment. He ate very little, and was terribly thin; the knowing ones among his fellow workers murmured : "T.B. or cancer." But there was surprising strength in his frail-looking body; it was his hatred which burned up his flesh.

He went into his tiny workshop. It had a brick floor, and underneath four loose bricks, deep in a little cavity close to the wall, was the bomb. The Algerians had assured him that it would keep for ever.

He stared at the spot, and planned how he would take up the bricks, and put the bomb in his pocket. He began to wonder where he would stand during the procession. Suddenly, he heard a sound and glanced round. His wife was in the doorway, staring, and he saw fear in her eyes.

"Matt—" she began chokily.

"What the devil are you doing here?"

"Matt, I—I saw you come out before breakfast. I didn't want you to catch cold. I—"

"You lying fool, you're spying on me! Go back into the house, put some clothes on, and stay there until I come back. Stay indoors! Do you understand?"

"I—I didn't meant to upset you, dear," his wife muttered, but she continued to stare. He did not realize how glittering his eyes were, or how his lips were drawn back over his teeth.

That had convinced her beyond doubt that something was hidden in this workshop. She had suspected it for a long time.

And she was more frightened than ever of her husband.

Beryl Belman was not frightened for herself. She had no idea that she had need to be. But she had.

8

SATURDAY ROLL-CALL

ON that same Saturday morning, Gideon was in his office a little after eight o'clock. Saturday was always the odds-and-ends day, a kind of roll-call of unsolved crimes. Gideon liked to go over all the jobs on which there had been no progress during the week, to see if he or the men in charge had missed anything obvious.

"Did you get hold of all the Provincial Supers I asked you to?" he asked Bell.

"Yes, George." Bell put his hand on a sheaf of letters. "They'll all play. They want someone to go and brief them on our bad boys, though, and I said we'd send someone up. Our chap can pick up a lot of information, too."

"Let me see the reports," Gideon said.

He read them closely, and by the time that and the morning briefing was done, it was ten o'clock.

"Going to have a breather for five minutes?" suggested Bell. "Lemaitre's coming at a quarter past, Evans is due from London Airport, and Abbott said he'd like to see you at half past eleven."

"Anything from Cox?"

"Not a squeak."

"Hmm," said Gideon. "All right, Joe, send for a cuppa." He got up, went to the window, and looked out, stretching himself and yawning. His collar was done up and his tie in position, for it was chilly. The windows were closed against a wind which seemed to have come in mistake for March, and was whipping up the surface of the Thames. He had been wrong as a weather prophet.

At a quarter past ten exactly there was a bang at the door, and Superintendent Lemaitre came in. For years Lemaitre had sat where Joe Bell did now. He was an old friend of Gideon's, a senior detective with one big fault, which somehow showed in his alert, thin-featured face and sounded in his Cockney voice, with its overtone of slick confidence.

"Hiyah, George!" He came in briskly, waved to Bell and added: "Joe," and shook Gideon's hand. "Just thought I'd come and put you out of your misery."

"What misery?"

"You won't have to come to Cornwall to do my job for me," announced Lemaitre. He sat on a corner of Gideon's desk, bony hands clenched, a confident and happy-looking man given to taking too much for granted and jumping to conclusions. "All three deaths were natural causes—I mean, all accidental drownings, George."

"Sure?"

"Yep. And I'm back full of the joys and ready for anything. Just had ten days down by the briny, all expenses paid—got in a couple of dips every day. My wife's so brown you wouldn't think she'd been decent! She wants to know if you and Kate can come round to tea or supper tomorrow."

"If Kate hasn't booked anything, we'd like to," said Gideon. "Then you can make your wife a police widow for a week or so."

"What's all this? I'm just the man you want for the Big Visit."

"So you are. Visits to Glasgow, Liverpool, Manchester, and the rest, to check whether any of their boys are planning an offensive in London during the Visit."

"Okay, okay," said Lemaitre, without a moment's hesitation. "I'll go. Heard anything about Sonnley, or Benny Klein?"

"Dimble of Manchester said he'd heard that Klein was up there," Bell put in.

"Buying the Manchester mobs off," Lemaitre guessed. "When do you want me to go?"

"Tuesday."

"Right-i-ho!" Lemaitre slapped his hands together.

"Won't be sorry to get out of this den of vice again. Don't forget to ask Kate about tomorrow."

As he went out, Abbott came in, looking rather over-eager; quite obviously he thought he had something to report, and couldn't wait. Lemaitre's footsteps clap-clapped down the corridor, as the door closed.

"Well, Abby?" Gideon asked.

"Eric Little was seen to pick up a girl at Swan and Edgar's on Tuesday night, just before the call went out for Marjorie Belman," Abbott said. "The girl answered Marjorie Belman's description. It's a belated report from a uniformed man, and I'm having the story checked. Might be the angle we're looking for."

If he had come in simply to report this, it was a bad sign. Gideon waited, concealing his disappointment, and then Abbott glanced at Bell, as if he wished the Chief Inspector wasn't there.

"Joe, nip along and get those letters from the typing pool for me," urged Gideon and winked.

Nothing flustered Joe Bell, who was not only self-effacing and competent, but a first-class second-in-command. As he went out, Gideon wondered, not for the first time, who would replace him, and shrugged the thought off.

"Something on your mind, Abby?"

"Yes," said Abbott. "Wasn't sure whether you'd want Joe in on it. Er—did you know I used to play a lot of tennis with Ray Cox?"

Gideon sat up, surprised.

"That's news to me."

"Well, I did. We were out at JI together for years. I—er—happen to know Ray's nose has been put out of joint. None of my business," Abbott went on hastily, "but he's been giving his Department hell this last day or two. He always was a bit tense. Thought you ought to know."

"That's a big help," said Gideon warmly. "Thanks."

"You won't let Ray know that I—er—warned you?"

"No one warned me."

"Thanks, George," Abbott said. "Well, I'll be on my way."

When he had gone, Gideon stared at the rain on the window, glad that Abbott's mind was working well, and wondering how he could get round Cox's antagonism. Warnings from Ripple and from Abbott must not be ignored. Before he reached any kind of conclusion, Bell came back, and at the same instant the telephone bell rang. Gideon picked up the telephone.

"That's probably Rip," said Bell. "He was due to call from Paris."

"Gideon speaking . . . yes, put him through." Gideon looked up at Bell. "Yes, it's him." He waited until Ripple's voice came. "Hallo, Rip. How's Paris?"

"They've put a bit of paint on since I was here last," said Ripple. "The Sûreté's got things laid on pretty well over here, too. Specially trained men will come with de Gaulle's party, and they'd like to send over about thirty of their chaps familiar with Algerian Colonists and Nationalists to have a look round. Have we any objecttions?"

"No. How will they come over? As tourists?"

"That's the idea. All unofficial."

"I'll fix it with Rogerson," promised Gideon. He talked for another couple of minutes, without learning any more, and replaced the receiver slowly.

"He expecting trouble?" asked Bell.

Gideon explained.

"Be a bit of a load off our backs," said Bell practically. "Better make sure how many will want accommodation, we don't want to have to give 'em bed and board here. They say that there's hardly a hotel room left in London for the week of the Visit. The Yanks are coming over in shiploads."

"Why not ask Miss Timson to book a hotel for these French chaps? That place over at Chelsea won't be any good, the Aussies will be back by then."

"Okay," said Bell, and immediately called Rogerson's

secretary. Gideon heard him draw in his breath, and for once Bell raised his voice.

"When the Assistant Commissioner's not in, you'll take your orders from the Commander. I don't care if it keeps you here all day." He rang off as angry as Gideon could remember seeing him. "The impertinent bitch."

"May be trouble between her and her boy-friend." Bell was the one man whom Gideon had told about the Australian and "Vi". To give Bell time to recover his temper, Gideon went on : "Joe, I'd forgotten the hotels and bars. There will be more con-men at work at the big hotels than we've had for a long time. Who've we got spare?"

Bell recovered and considered.

"Parsons," he came up with, at last. "He knows London hotels as well as anyone."

"See if he's in," ordered Gideon.

Parsons was a chubby, jolly, happy-looking man, with a smooth skin and a ready tongue. He listened to Gideon for ten minutes before he said :

"I've got it, skipper. We want every hotel detective on the look out for suspect con-men, and we want a few of our chaps spread around pretty thin, because we can't spare many. Mind if I make a suggestion?"

"Go ahead."

"Might be a good idea to have New York, Washington, Paris and Bonn send over photographs of any of their missing con-men, so we can distribute the pictures to the hotels."

"Do that," approved Gideon.

It was half past six in London, and in New York the time was about half past one. The door of the Police Commissioner's office at Headquarters opened and a tall, slim man in a pale grey suit came in, without any of Lemaitre's kind of bustle.

The Commissioner looked up.

"You heard anything new?" he demanded.

"I've heard enough to make me think that O'Hara's flown to London, and that could mean he's going to try to kill the President there," the young man answered. "I think it's time we informed Washington."

"That's exactly what I'll do, Jed," the Commissioner said.

Gideon still had that restless feeling, and wished that he could go out on a job himself instead of leaving them all to others. Abbott and Cox between them were on his mind, and he was uneasy in case concentration on the plans for the Visit should make him slip up on one of the more immediate jobs.

There was no doubt that Abbott was seriously worried about the Belman girl, and it would be easy to put that down to Abbot's lack of confidence. But supposing he was right? Should Gideon have made a great effort to trace the girl? He was still brooding about Marjorie Belman when he heard footsteps outside, and looked up at once : for these were the footsteps of a man in a hurry. There was a perfunctory tap at the door before it opened, and Abbott stood dramatically on the threshold. Abbott's news showed in his over-bright eyes and his pale cheeks. It was almost an anti-climax when he said :

"They've found Marjorie Belman, drowned off Sandown in the Isle of Wight. That swine got her."

Gideon said very slowly : "Have we got Carraway?"

"He's over at his main showrooms. I've sent a Q car to watch him."

"Come on," Gideon said, and stood up. "Let's go and see him."

9

KILLER?

IT was like being released from solitary confinement.

Gideon strode along the passages of the Yard with Abbott a pace behind him, and men saw him and stood hasily aside, or watched covertly from half-open doors. The word went round : "Gee-Gee's on the rampage." There were sighs of relief when he headed for the lift, and the main door. His car, with a chauffeur at the wheel, was pulling up at the foot of the steps : Bell had lost no time.

"Hop in," Gideon said to Abbott. "Tell me about it on the way."

All there was to tell were the bare facts, reported by the police from Sandown. Abbott hardly knew whether to blame himself for the girl's death, or to feel vindicated. The chauffeur, slowing down as lights changed to amber, felt the back of his seat move as Gideon gripped it, and boomed :

"Get a move on."

"Right, sir."

Traffic seemed to fall aside for them. Policemen who recognized Gideon's car kept the evening crowds at bay. They swept along Whitehall, along Haymarket to Piccadilly, and round to Regent Street, then to Portman Place. Five minutes before he had expected Gideon saw the big new garage, painted a pale pink, with the name *Carraway Car Sales and Rentals*.

Thirty or forty new-looking cars with price labels were parked alongside the petrol pumps, where two boys were busy with petrol. The car pulled up near the showrooms, in which new cars were standing, with *Immediate Delivery* signs over the windscreens. Gideon got out of one door and Abbott the other, on the instant. Gideon caught sight of a glossy-haired, stocky little man talking to a tall woman—and saw the way this man stared at Abbott, and how he looked across at a door marked : *Office*. Gideon did not know it then, but this man was Eric Little. He had no time to warn Carraway before Gideon and Abbott reached the door, which Gideon pushed wider open. Carraway was sitting at a flat-topped desk, in his shirt sleeves, cigarette dangling from his lips. He looked immaculate.

"What the hell—" he began, and then appeared to see Abbott for the first time. His lips tightened, his eyes narrowed.

Gideon growled : "Mr. Carraway?"

"I'm busy. Can't you— ?"

A telephone bell rang on his desk. Carraway stretched out for it, but Abbott moved swftly, took it first, and said into the telephone :

"I'm afraid he's busy. Will you call him back?" and rang off.

"You've got a nerve," Carraway said roughly. His eyes were still narrowed, but he had shown no outward signs of fright. "Who are you?"

"I'm Commander Gideon of New Scotland Yard. When did you last see Marjorie Belman?"

"What the hell's that got to do with you?" Carraway demanded.

He certainly wasn't going to be easy; in fact he was going to be a hard man to beat. It was already easy to understand why Abbott was unsure of himself. Gideon glanced out of the window and saw the glossy-haired man driving off in a car, with the woman beside him. The couple would be followed, and if he was demonstrating a car it would make no difference. Two more Yard men were in sight already.

"Answer my question, please," Gideon said.

"Why the devil should I?"

"Try answering it."

"Now you listen to me," Carraway said coldly. He pushed his chair back from the desk, squashed out his cigarette, and stood up. He spared a glance almost of derision for Abbott, then looked back to Gideon. "I don't care if you're the Commissioner of the Metropolitan Police himself, no one's going to burst into my office like that and get away with it. I had enough trouble with Abbott over the murder of my partner. I don't want any more over a skirt."

"When did you last see her?"

"I tell you—"

"All right, Abby," Gideon said roughly. "Let's take him along to the Yard. Call the others—"

Abbott stepped to the window, and raised his right hand. A man standing at the far end of the rows of cars came forward; another followed him. Gideon saw Carraway lose a little colour, and moisten his lips momentarily, but that was his only sign of weakness.

"I can't waste time going to the Yard. I've got a lot of work to do. I haven't seen Marjorie Belman for days."

"How many days?"

Carraway said: "Three or four."

"How about Tuesday night?"

"I didn't see her Tuesday night," declared Carraway. The other two Yard men were at the window, waiting for a signal from Gideon. "I was working late. Ever since Rawson died I've worked late every night. I'm trying to do two men's work."

"Can you prove you didn't see Marjorie Belman that night?"

Carraway exploded: "Why the hell should I? Why—?" he broke off, paled again, hesitated, and then stared at Gideon as if worried for the first time: he was very, very clever. "What's happened to her? What's the matter?"

"Sure you don't know?"

"Just tell me what it's all about, and I'll tell you what I can."

Gideon did not know why he evaded the question as he did; there was something of a sixth sense in his move, that sense which made him so much more able than most

75

detectives. He knew that Abbott would not interrupt or give him away, and he said :

"She's been missing since Wednesday evening."

"Missing," echoed Carraway. "Didn't she go home?"

"You didn't exactly encourage her to, did you?"

"Listen, Mr. Gideon," Carraway said, "this isn't an inquiry into my morals, is it? The kid wanted a gay life, so I gave her one. If she'd known what was good for her she would have stayed with me. But her family nagged at her, and finally she gave up. She told me she was going back to them."

"Did you quarrel with her?"

"I don't quarrel with hysterical kids," Carraway sneered. "While she was sensible, she was okay." He moistened his lips again. "Er—didn't she go back home?"

"She's not been seen for three and a half days. Unless you've seen her."

"I haven't set eyes on her," Carraway insisted. "The last time I saw her was Monday. She'd had a talk with a sister, who'd been sent round by Ma and Pa, and the session upset her. I tried to calm her down, but she wasn't having any, so I told her if she preferred living like a nun, it was okay by me. I walked out of the flat I rented for her when she said she was going back home." He frowned. "Are you sure — ?"

After a pause, Gideon said : "I'm sure." He stood looking at Carraway intently, twice as powerful as the motorcar salesman, and then nodded and said : "If you hear from her, let us know at once."

He turned and led the way out, Abbott nearly stumbling over his heels, and then looked round sharply ; but Carraway's expression hadn't changed.

The man with the glossy black hair, an Italian type, was driving back into the garage with the woman still by his side.

"That's Eric Little," Abbott volunteered. "Want to talk to him?"

"Not now," Gideon said, and climbed into his car. He waited for Abbott to join him, and the doors slammed.

"He's going to be a tough nut," he declared. "Don't let up on him, Abby."

"Believe me I won't," said Abbott. "But, George—" He was getting bold.

"Hmm?"

"He didn't bat an eyelid."

"He didn't bat enough eyelids," Gideon growled. "He put on his poker face too soon."

He knew that a weaker man than Carraway would probably have given himself away under the weight of that sudden pressure; and he felt quite sure, as Abbott did, that Carraway knew exactly what he was about. It would probably be best to attack him through one of his salesmen, now—Little, for instance; and he must be followed wherever he went in an effort to break his nerve.

In spite of the failure to make Carraway give anything away, Gideon felt better; the little flurry of action had done him good. It would also do Abbott good, in the long run, to know that he wasn't failing on an easy job.

Abbott already seemed rather more confident of himself.

"Don't you worry," he said, quietly. "I'll make sure he's watched. Why didn't you tell him she was dead?"

"Let's keep him on the hook a bit," Gideon advised. "His defences were up too soon. We need a bit more evidence."

"I'll get some evidence," Abbott said grimly. "I'll keep Little and the others on the hook, too, and try to make them squirm."

Soon after Gideon and Abbott left the office, Eric Little brought the middle-aged woman back to sign a hire purchase agreement. The woman was rather too self-confident and loud-voiced. Carraway let her take control of the situation, witnessed the agreement, took her cheque, and watched her drive out of the garage. She was seen off by Little. Then he shrugged his arms into his coat, went out and met Little between the roadway and the office. He hardly moved his lips as he said :

77

"They don't know she's dead. Watch yourself, they might be tailing you." In a loud voice, he went on : "If I don't get a drink, I'll break a blood vessel. You take over."

He walked on.

On the Saturday evening, about the same time, Eric Little shook hands with a plump man who had just signed a hire purchase agreement for an Austin Cambridge, and escorted him to the door of the showrooms. Then he went back, and picked up each of the two London evening papers, early editions, which were on his desk. Each had advertisements for the company's rental and for sale, but he was much more interested in news about Marjorie's body. The body of "a young woman in her early twenties" had been found off Sandown on the Isle of Wight, but the police, according to the report, hadn't yet been able to identify it.

"It's as safe as houses," he told himself, and remembered how the two Yard men had been rebuffed. Carraway certainly kept his nerve, and that was all there was to it. Strong nerves. If that damned sister hadn't come round—

He saw a girl walking past the petrol pumps towards the door. At first, he felt as if someone had stuck a knife into him, it was such a shock. That walk. That hair. He stood by the desk, white-faced and with his hands shaking as he lit a cigarette ; then the girl stepped out of the shadow of the cover over the pumps, and he saw that the likeness was only a passing one.

But for that moment he had thought that this was Marjorie Belman, come back to life.

The girl hesitated outside the door, looking in. Little was placed in such a position that he could see out, but could not be seen—he always liked to make sure that he could vet callers first. When standing still, as when walking, this girl was uncannily like Marjorie. The cigarette burned Little's tongue because he drew in the smoke so deeply.

It must be the sister. He hadn't seen her clearly the other night, but—who else could it be?

She came in, looking round. Near her was a bell-push marked *Inquiries*. Little moistened his lips, stubbed out the cigarette in a large ash-tray, and stood up. The girl saw him. Her eyes were very like Marjorie's, too, but her complexion was much fairer—and now that she was closer he saw that her hair was dark brown. There was another difference; she had more of a figure than the dead girl— was much fuller at the breast.

"Good afternoon," Little said, as breezily as he could. "Can I help you?"

She looked at him appraisingly. His heart was thumping, he still felt the effect of that uncanny likeness, and he knew cold fear; but she showed no sign of recognition.

"I'm Beryl Belman," she announced.

He played dumb.

"Who?"

"Marjorie Belman's sister," the girl said flatly.

He had to say something, he had to recover from the shock.

"Good Lord," he exclaimed. "Jorrie's sister!"

"That's right," said Beryl Belman, solemnly. "Her older sister."

"I didn't even know she had one."

"Will you please tell me where she is?"

Little was feeling better now, and beginning to think clearly. If she had seen him the other night she would have said something about it by now, so there was no emergency—yet.

"Isn't she at her flat?"

"No. I've just come from there."

"Well—*I* don't know where she is," Little declared. "No—no idea. I know she is a friend of my managing director, but he's not at this branch today. I'll ask him to let you know if he has any idea where Jorrie is, shall I? Eh? Can I—can I get in touch with you?"

He offered cigarettes. When Beryl Belman didn't appear to notice them, Little took one himself, his fingers unsteady.

"Sure you won't have a cigarette?"

"I don't smoke," she said flatly.

Now she was staring at him even more intently. It was almost as if she was wondering where she had seen him before, as if she was accusing him.

"Well, er, if you'll tell me where I can get in touch with you, I'll ask my boss if he can help," Little offered.

"Where can I see him?"

"He travels about so much that you can never be sure."

"I want to talk to him. I've telephoned him twice, but he's been out each time. I want to talk to him about my sister."

Little replied calmly : "Your sister was quite old enough to look after herself, you know. She—" He realized suddenly that he had said "*your sister was*", and for a terrible moment thought that this girl would realize the significance of the slip, but she did not seem to be alarmed. "I mean, she's over twenty-one, she can do what she likes."

"I don't want to argue with you," said Beryl, "but I intend to see Bruce Carraway. He may not realize it, but he's broken my mother's heart, and my father's terribly upset, too. I've got to see Marjorie and make her come back home. I've been along to her flat twice a day since last Tuesday, and there's no answer. One of the cleaners said that a man was there last night, but that she hasn't seen Marjorie, and—I want to know if Carraway *has* cast her aside."

The words came out so quietly that they carried tragedy, not pathos, even when she went on :

"Has he? If he has, she's got to realize that Mum and Dad will forgive her. All they want is for her to come back."

Little was feeling much better, virtually certain that she hadn't recognized him, confident that he could handle the situation.

"I don't think there's been any trouble between Jorrie

and my boss," he said. "But I haven't seen her for a couple of weeks or more."

Beryl Belman looked astonished: "Of course you have!"

"Now look here, young lady," said Little almost playfully, "are you calling me a liar?"

"You saw her last Tuesday evening, and took her off in a car," asserted Beryl sharply. "I'd been to her flat, and followed her to Piccadilly. I saw her go off with you."

The words sounded like a death-knell to Eric Little, each one booming sonorously inside his head. It was an awful sound, with a terrible significance which he could not fail to see. If this girl ever talked to the police, he would be caught for murder.

He thought: *I've got to get rid of her*.

Beryl thought: *He's lying to me*.

And she thought: *He looks like the man I saw at Jorrie's place, but I can't be sure*.

Her heart was beating very fast as she waited for him to make some comment, for no man liked being called a liar. Other thoughts passed rapidly through her mind, the most important that she had to find out where Jorrie was, and that this man might be able to help her. She was scared, and yet determined, as she stared defiantly into the man's sallow but rather good-looking face. He kept moving his lips without opening his mouth, and she assumed that he was trying to keep a hold on his temper.

Before he spoke, Beryl said:

"It's no use pretending. I *did* see you."

"All—all right," said Little, and his lips parted in a tense smile; she did not notice that there was no smile in his eyes. "I can't fool you, I can see." He rubbed his nose with a sharp, vigorous action. "As a matter of fact—"

A car turned in from the main road, and moved fast towards him; it was one of the other salesmen. He glanced round. He saw no policeman, so apparently they had gone after Carraway. He waved to the newcomer, a kind of "keep off" gesture, and the other grinned and went jauntily into the saleroom. Heavy traffic was passing along the road, often very fast.

"Listen," said Little. "We can't talk here, we're bound to be interrupted, and I've got a customer coming in five minutes' time. How about meeting me later?"

"I want to know where my sister is," Beryl said firmly. "I'm not going to be put off."

"Don't you worry, I'll tell you all I can," he assured her. She could not make up her mind whether he was lying or telling the truth. "It's a bit complicated, and — well, Carraway's my boss, see, I've got to watch myself." She saw sweat on his forehead. "We close at half past eight. How about meeting me at Hampstead Heath at nine o'clock?"

"I don't know Hampstead Heath very well," Beryl objected quickly.

"That's all right, we can meet somewhere central," said Little hastily. "How about by the pond? You can get there by bus. The easy way is to go to Swiss Cottage and walk. We can have a talk, and —"

"*Do* you know where Jorrie is?"

Little said: "As a matter of fact, I'm a bit worried about her. I don't think Carraway's playing the game by her. But — listen, I can't talk here, my customer's just arrived."

A scarlet MG car swung off the road, a young man with snowy fair hair driving, and a girl with a mop of shiny black hair sitting beside him. They looked handsome and attractive. The driver raised a hand in greeting to the man with Beryl, and she realized that there was no chance to talk now; all that mattered was making this man tell her where to find Jorrie.

"Will you be there?" the man demanded.

"I — yes, all right, but you'd better have news for me."

"I'll have news," he assured her. He gripped her hand, and gave a forced smile. "Don't worry, I'll have news for you." He turned away and walked hurriedly towards the snowy-haired driver and his companion. The girl was sitting at ease with an arm stretched along the back of the bench seat. "Good evening, Mr. Armstrong," the sales-man said, his voice carrying clearly. "I've got that Bristol ready . . ."

It was half past seven, so there was plenty of time—too much time. With a sense of eagerness and excitement which she had not known before, Beryl left the showroom. It looked as if she was going to get what she wanted. It wouldn't be long now.

"I tell you she saw me, she can put a finger on me," Little said huskily. He was in the office, just before half past eight, and Carraway was sitting at his desk, his jacket on now, looking as if he had just come from his tailor. "We've got to keep her quiet, can't you see?"

"We haven't got to keep anyone quiet," Carraway said.

"What the hell do you mean?"

"Listen, Eric," Carraway said, and leaned forward, staring up into the other's eyes. "You're in trouble. *I'm* not. The only witness who could have caught me out on the Rawson job is dead, and you killed her. You laid it all on. *I* didn't touch her. I hadn't seen her for days. I wasn't anywhere near Brighton or the South coast, and I can prove it. Don't get anything wrong. I'm not in any trouble."

Little stood, half crouching, his body so rigid that it was almost as if it had turned to stone. The only vivid sign of life was in his burning eyes.

"I was playing poker with you and the others on the night Rawson was murdered, and the others will stick to that story," Carraway went on. "Understand that? If you try to back out now, I'll say that you're trying to frame me. The police might question me, they might even charge me, but they couldn't make the charge stick. You could talk till you're blue in the face and it wouldn't be any use to them as evidence."

Little said, in a queer, grating voice : "You paid me—a thousand quid."

"For commission, Eric, for commission! We've had a damned good season, in spite of the slump. I paid the others a thousand quid each, too. After all, fair's fair. You're in trouble all right, but you can get yourself out. Don't try to drag me into it, that's all." He gave a short, high-pitched laugh. "Why, it was you who went to Jorrie's apartment and started getting her clothes together! I was right out at Wimbledon at the time, and can prove it. Just get yourself out of trouble, Eric, and don't expect any help from me."

"Why, you—you *swine*."

"You don't have to worry," Carraway said, smoothly. "You've got a good job, and you'll always get a fat bonus while you work for me. All you have to do is keep yourself out of trouble—like you have before. Just think what your wife and kids would feel like if you got topped for kill-ing—"

"*Keep your bloody mouth shut!*" Little screeched.

"I'm only telling you," said Carraway. Then he leaned forward and went on earnestly: "You've got a lot to thank me for, Eric. The cops are after me, not you. They're not interested in you yet. You've got plenty of time to do what you want to do. Why don't you use that time? I'm going to have a nice little drive out to Watford. That will keep them busy, radio patrol cars and all. While I'm leading them up the garden, you've got plenty of time to shut that little bitch's mouth."

10

SHADOW

ERIC LITTLE stepped out of Carraway's office, almost blinded with rage, but as he walked across to the cars, his heels smacking against the macadam, fear began to creep up on him : fear of what that girl's evidence could do. By the time he reached his car, he realized beyond doubt that Carraway was right. The slimy, cunning swine had fixed things so that nothing could be proved against him ; he had swung the whole load on to Little's shoulders.

Little almost choked.

He had to get rid of that girl.

He sat in the car for a few minutes, drawing fiercely at a cigarette. It was twenty-five to nine. The other salesmen had gone home, only Carraway and the petrol pump attendants were on the premises, and he did not think that Carraway would come out yet.

He was a devil.

One sentence he had uttered burned itself into Little's mind : *"Just think what your wife and kids would feel like if you got topped for killing—"*

Nora and the kids, the triplets, Beth, Jane and Bob. He had killed once to save his home and his family, and Carraway knew that it was the one all-consuming love of his life. Somehow he couldn't help playing around with other girls, but he was never serious and Nora never knew. Nora mustn't know.

Why the hell had he allowed Carraway to make him kill Jorrie?

It did not matter how often he asked the question, the answer was always the same : not for money, at least not only for the money, not because of the earlier murder, because he would do anything to save his home.

85

Now he had to go and see—*now he had to go and kill*—Beryl Belman.

He tossed the cigarette out of the window, started the engine, and drove with more than usual care on to the main road, where the traffic had slackened. Then he turned towards Swiss Cottage. He could be at the Pond in ten minutes, and might arrive before the girl. He didn't want that, he wanted to draw up alongside her, tell her to step in, and make sure that no one standing around could identify him. He could change the number plates on the car in the morning; there was no danger from that.

He drove slowly as far as Swiss Cottage and up the hill towards the Heath to the Pond.

A few children were still playing with boats in the dusk, and the lights of a dozen cars were reflected in the water. Several adults were standing around, idly. A man went hurrying up to a girl, and they flung their arms round each other, as if life depended on their meeting.

Beryl wasn't here.

Little drove down towards the village, and it was then that he noticed the Rover. Shocked, he remembered that the police often drove Rovers. It was fairly close behind him, and although he gave it two chances to pass, the driver preferred to lag behind. Now Little's heart began to pound. He peered into his mirror, and made out the heads and shoulders of two men in the front of the car; both big men who might be from the Yard. He could not see them well enough to be sure, but who else would follow him? He turned a corner without giving a signal; and the Rover came after him but made no attempt to catch up.

Words burst from his lips: "They're after me."

He was in a panic for several minutes, wanting to pull up and to give himself a chance to think, wanting to make sure that these men were detectives. He slowed down to ten miles an hour—so did the other car. There was no reasonable doubt that they were detectives.

That girl would be waiting for him by now.

The police mustn't see him with her; if they once saw him with her they would start asking questions and she

86

would talk, just as Jorrie would have. He was sweating and half choking as he drove on, fighting for self-control, trying to make himself think clearly.

If he didn't turn up at the Pond, the girl would probably go to the police. The danger was acute. He must stop her somehow—oh, God, what should he do? And what would the police think of him, driving around like this? He had to fool them. It could be life and death. As he began to reason with himself, he felt better, and slowly evolved a practical plan. He must drive to a corner fairly close to the Pond, park the car, give the impression that he was waiting for someone, then make a rush for the Pond and the girl. He must put her off somehow, without being seen with her; that was the only chance.

He waited until five past nine, then pulled up near the gates of a big private house. He parked for a few minutes before getting out and walking up and down. The men sat and waited for him, without troubling to get out, as if they believed that he would be all right while near his car. He strolled as far as the corner of the street, turned as if casually, then swung round again and made a rush for the Pond. He did not see whether he was followed, just raced towards the spot itself. He saw Beryl waiting, looking about her. She saw him coming. He rushed up to her, now walking very fast, and before she could speak he burst out:

"I can't wait now, Carraway's following me. Call me at the garage, Monday. I'm on Jorrie's trail. Ask for Eric Little."

Then he left her standing.

An hour later, the Rover turned into the street where Little lived, in Hendon, a street of modern houses, with the lamps alight and windows aglow. He turned his car into the garage and got out. He had decided what to say to Nora if the police came to ask him questions; he would put all the blame on to Carraway. He felt better, as he always did when he had time to think.

He let himself in, and the living-room door opened. Nora, tall, fair, willowy, appeared against the light.

"Is that you, Eric?"

"Yes, pet, I'm sorry—"

"Don't make a sound, they've only just got off to sleep."

"I won't make a sound," Little promised.

He felt much, much better an hour later, for the police had not called on him, and the Rover had disappeared from the street, He had won another chance to make sure that Beryl Belman could never give evidence against him.

Beryl knew only that the black-haired man had looked scared, and that frightened her, too. She took it for granted that he was frightened by Carraway, and if Carraway could have that effect on a man, what could he do to Jorrie?

She could wait until Monday, anyhow, ask for Eric Little, and see what he had to say. If she got no results she would have to make herself confront Carraway. But it would be far better if she could find out from the other man where Jorrie was.

The fear which entered her head about Jorrie, the obvious explanation of her disappearance, did not really shock Beryl, but just made her feel miserable because of the effect it would have on her mother and father.

Supposing Jorrie was going to have a baby?

11

TWO MEN WALK

Just after ten o'clock next morning, Sunday, the telephone bell rang in Gideon's house. Two of his daughters were in the kitchen, finishing the washing-up, and young Malcolm was scurrying through his week-end task of peeling the potatoes and apples for lunch, not exactly resentful of the chore, but with a thirteen-year-old's impatience. Kate was bustling about upstairs, making the beds. It was a heavy, muggy day. The grass was dripping with moisture, the windows were streaked, and unless the sun broke through there would be no chance of working in the garden. Gideon was sitting in the front room, a Sunday custom, with the newspapers. He turned to the gardening notes of the *Express* as the bell rang.

Sleeves rolled up, shirt collar undone, Gideon strolled into the hall, where one of the telephones was.

It was Abbott to report fully on the pathologist's report on Marjorie Belman. Abbott was much more incisive than usual; he had taken the girl's death hard, and blamed himself for letting her disappear. The consequence seemed to be an even greater determination to catch her killer.

"Yes, it was murder all right. There's a scratch on her shoulder, probably where she was held under water. Her bikini was put on after death—scratch marks make that clear. That's official."

"What do you want me to do?" asked Gideon.

"I need to know whether Carraway or one of his three stooges has a big ring on either hand," said Abbott. "Shall I call the Yard about it?"

"I'll call 'em," Gideon said. "I want to check whether anything's in, anyhow."

Information told him that there had been no major

crimes during the night, and that there should be no difficulty about getting the information about any of Carraway's men who wore a ring. As Gideon finished, Kate came downstairs briskly, turning at the foot of the stairs with an unconscious grace which Gideon noticed much more these days.

"You haven't got to go to the office, have you?" She looked anxious.

"Day off, I should say," said Gideon. "Kate, I'd like to go up to town this afternoon. Have you anything fixed, or will you come?"

Kate's eyes lit up.

"No, do you want an early lunch?"

"One-ish."

"I'll go and see how those girls are getting on," said Kate, and hurried along to the kitchen.

Gideon heard the three of them talking, then laughing. There was something reassuring and satisfying about a happy family, and these days his could hardly be happier, although ten years ago the marriage could have gone on the rocks. Rocks. He thought of the three drowned girls in Cornwall, and now the drowned Marjorie Belman, whom he had never seen, but who had been eager and alive on Tuesday—certainly as recently as last Tuesday.

He thought, as he so often did, of the impenetrable fog of London; of the secrets it held; the horrors it could cover; the fear that lurked in many places; the death that threatened. For four days Marjorie Belman had been dead, and there had been a moment when she had realized that she was about to be murdered, an awful moment of dread and horror and pain.

How many others had suffered?

How many had died? How many bodies would be found, this week, next week, even in a few weeks' or a few months' time? Too many. And how many men were sitting in a pub, or at their own breakfast table, or reading the newspapers, and plotting the crimes for next week and next month? How many were cashing in on the Visit, for instance, or planning to?

He left with Kate soon after two o'clock, well fed on roast beef. Kate was wearing a summer weight suit of small black and white check, black shoes, white gloves and black handbag. She looked fresh and contented.

"I thought we'd have a drive along the procession route, and walk back," said Gideon. "We can pick up a cab back to the car if we feel like it. Then how about tea at the Dorchester?"

"Sounds lovely and expensive," said Kate.

She watched him when they reached Buckingham Palace, approaching it from Victoria and Birdcage Walk. His large hands were very square and firm on the wheel. He anticipated where other cars would go, and what they would do, so well that no other vehicle drew too close. He had to crawl round Trafalgar Square, where a band was playing. When it stopped, a man's voice came over the loud-speaker.

"What's happening here today?" asked Kate.

"Some kind of drive to help refugees," Gideon said. "Haven't got a thousand, have they? Give them a Ban the Bomb meeting, or an anti-something hate campaign, and we wouldn't be able to move. Like to stretch your legs for a minute?"

A few people were sitting by the bronze lions. There was a thick crowd near the Strand, beseiged by the pigeons. The man was still talking; a dozen banners were being held high, as the Gideons listened.

Kate felt Gideon's hand tighten on hers. "Look straight ahead," he whispered, but before she could stop herself she glanced around, and noticed a tall, lean man with angular square shoulders, walking with an absurdly short woman by his side, and a boy of nine or ten. Gideon stared straight ahead. Kate saw the man glance round, too, and saw him react, much as her husband had done. She caught his eye, and because she had no idea who it was, and suspected a man on the Yard's blacklist, she looked away.

91

"See that man in the green hat and brown suit?" asked Gideon, when they were back in the car.

"With the tiny woman and the boy?"

"That's Ray Cox," said Gideon. "I pretended not to notice him. Last thing I want is to make him think I'm watching him all the time."

"You're a bit worried about Cox, aren't you, George?"

"I suppose I am a bit."

Had Kate pressed the subject he would not really have been able to say why.

"Did you see that?" demanded Cox.

"What, dear?" asked Mildred.

"Gideon."

"Commander Gideon?"

"Yes, Mr. Commander Gideon," said Cox in a hard voice. "He cut me dead, and his wife snubbed me, too."

"Ray!" Mildred glanced down at their son, who was looking up with keen interest. Then she went on: "Perhaps he didn't notice you, dear. He's probably doing the same as you, spying out the ground."

"Spying," Cox echoed, and laughed without humour. "That's about it."

On that beautiful Sunday afternoon, half London seemed to be patrolling the route for the Visit. Gideon did not see them, but Alec Sonnley and his Rosie walked the length of the route, Rosie sighing about her poor feet, Sonnley whistling softly. Lumati had a stand near Trafalgar Square—outside the National Gallery—where he did his lightning portraits for ten shillings each, and was seen earning this honest living by at least a dozen men from the Yard, including Cox. Matthew Smith walked the route with his wife, who was willing to do anything to placate him; he was desperately anxious to select the perfect spot for throwing his bomb. Now and again the realization that he would soon strike the final blow for the memory of his son affected him so that his eyes took on that glittering frightening expression. He did not realize this physical change : but Grace, his wife, did.

Carraway wasn't in the heart of London, but Little, his wife, and three children were, and actually passed the Belmans, father and mother. Belman had persuaded "mother" to come with him, in another effort to shake her out of herself, but she walked along as if in a daze, saying "Yes," and "No," and "Really!" whenever he tried to spark her interest. Beryl was at home doing her smalls and washing her hair.

Gideon and Kate were back at their car when a plain-clothes man came up, gave a half-timid grin at Kate, and reported :

"There's a message for you, sir. Will you telephone the Commissioner at his house when convenient ?"

That was a rare request.

"I'll call as soon as I can," Gideon promised, and a few minutes later pulled up near Westminster Bridge Station. He left Kate in the car, and called Scott-Marle's home number from a call-box.

"Oh, Gideon. Thank you for calling." Scott-Marle paused for a moment, then went on, in his clear, precise way : "I have had an urgent call from Washington. A man named O'Hara is known to have flown from New York to London yesterday morning, and Washington thinks he might try to harm the President when he is here next month. Will you start a search for this O'Hara ?"

"I'll get it started at once," Gideon promised. His voice gave no indication of the way his heart lurched; this was the kind of development he most feared.

"I'll be glad if you will," said Scott-Marle.

Gideon still covered his feelings when he went back, said : "Sorry, Kate. You'd better sit here and watch the river. I've got a job that will take twenty minutes or so."

"I'll be all right, dear," Kate assured him.

In fact, it took Gideon half an hour to brief some of Ripple's men, and to start inquiries at the London airport. Once it was done, he felt better. At least they were forewarned. The Special Branch men would get a dossier on this O'Hara from Washington, probably from the Federal Bureau of Investigation, and the airport police would start the long, painstaking and often futile task of checking back on passengers. Washington would always fuss over the President, but by naming the man O'Hara, they showed how worried they were.

Gideon went back to the car and tried to put this new anxiety out of his mind.

Kate looked inquiringly, and he said : "Washington wants some special precautions," and left it at that.

He drove back to a street leading from Birdcage Walk to Victoria Street, and parked. It was still warm, but the sun was dodging behind clouds as they walked along to Parliament Square, then up to Whitehall. At Trafalgar Square they crossed the road and walked on the other side, towards the Houses of Parliament, passed the little street leading to the Yard, and stopped at the corner approaching the Houses of Parliament.

"Here's another danger spot," he said. "Just imagine what could happen if a lunatic threw a bomb from here."

"It might kill a dozen people !" Kate sounded shocked.

"That's the second big worry," said Gideon. "We can be reasonably sure of saving anyone in the procession, but a man with a nitro-glycerine bomb, or even dynamite, could injure a lot of bystanders."

Deep down in his mind, that worry was as great as any ; the consequences of any attempt at assassination among the crowd could be dreadful. It was a half-formed fear, a dread which drove him to even greater precautions, greater thoroughness. More than ever he wished that he could cut through the barrier which seemed to him to have become erected between him and Cox.

"Very well, as we've come this far, let's go into the Abbey," said Matthew Smith to his wife. He was smiling to himself, calmer now because he had selected the exact place from which he was going to stand and throw his bomb—from the pavement in front of a big stand, already being erected. Grace felt momentarily happier, too, because he seemed more content, but her underlying anxiety remained.

Abbott came up from Brighton but did not go near the crowds that Sunday. He spent his time at the Yard.

In the afternoon, he learned that Donald Atkinson, one of Carraway's salesmen, habitually wore a ring. At twenty past four, he was told that Eric Little, the chief salesman, also wore one. Carraway himself did not.

Before long, Abbott knew, the fact that Marjorie Belman had been found drowned would have to be released, but he believed that the right tactics were to play cat-and-mouse with Carraway, Little and the man Atkinson. It would make little if any difference to the girl's parents; they would endure another day or two of uncertainty, that was all. From all he heard, the sister was a nice kid, but the young were seldom affected so much as the old.

If Gideon would agree, Abbott decided to stall a while longer.

On that Sunday, in Glasgow, another and very different kind of crime was being considered, one which made Benny Klein and Jock Gorra, of the Glasgow Blacks, feel very pleased with themselves. They had hatched out the plot together—one man who had been adopted by Great Britain and given its nationality, the other the leader of one of the most vicious of the gangs north of the Tweed. Their plan was simple, and depended entirely on perfect timing. Instead of Sonny Boy Sonnley's pickpockets and bag snatchers being busy during the Visit, the Glasgow Blacks would descend on London in strength.

Whenever they had done this in the past there had been a clash with the London crooks, often a pitched battle. Each side had brought its gangs as reinforcements, and usually the fights were broken up by the police.

Klein had said, and Gorra had agreed, that this was a crazy way to go on.

"All you want to do is put Sonny Boy's artists out of

action for a few days," Klein had said. "Then London's wide open."

"You're telling me what to do, now just tell me how." Gorra was a thickset man with a small, round head covered with a gingery bristle. His short, pale eyelashes and stubby eyebrows made him look almost like an albino; his pale blue eyes seemed to stare all the time.

"You ever seen a dip or a bagman work with burned fingers?" Klein had inquired smoothly.

At first that had not made sense to Gorra, but the light had soon dawned. They were working out a way to burn the fingers of Sonnley's artists, and Klein was on a winner: acid would do the trick, a nice hot, corrosive acid.

The only question was how to get it on to the right fingers.

12

EFFICIENCY

On Monday morning, there was a thick file on Gideon's desk, marked: *"Proposals for Special Occasion—Uniformed Branch."* Bell was on the telephone, and the report was on the top of a pile. Gideon leafed through it. In a small, meticulous handwriting were detailed proposals for the whole of the State Procession. With it was a sketch map of the area, taken from previous processions, and marked in red were those points which Cox suggested should be barricaded off. Wooden fences with small doors would be erected; the Office of Works would require details soon. Cox was right on the ball.

Gideon took out his own files, and checked.

"Victoria Street, police cordon." On the map, police cordons were marked in broken blue lines. *"Whitehall approach from Great Scotland Yard—barricades both sides."* Good. Gideon's lips moved as he checked, until at last he came to the last entry: *"To regulate traffic more effectively, it is recommended that the approaches to Westminster and Lambeth Bridges be cordoned off."* This was new, but at first sight wise; every big occasion brought more and more traffic into the city.

Bell stopped talking into the telephone and put it down.

"'Morning, George."

"'Morning, Joe. When did this thing come in from Cox?"

"It was here when I arrived."

"He must have been at it all the week-end."

"And couldn't wait to show you how good he was."

Gideon looked at Bell sharply.

"He been needling you?"

"I met him in the corridor. He just acknowledged that I exist."

"Can't see what else has rubbed him up the wrong way," Gideon said, and rubbed the shiny bowl of the big pipe in his pocket. He seldom smoked it, but it was a kind of touchstone. "Have you seen this?"

"Seems a good job."

Gideon didn't answer.

"Isn't it?" asked Bell.

"As far as it goes, yes."

"Where doesn't it go?"

"Far enough. He's forgotten the plans at the airport on arrival, the routes to the embassies and hotels, and the periods before and after the actual Procession."

Bell rubbed a stubbly chin.

"I missed them, too," he admitted, ruefully. "Couldn't see the trees for the wood. Think he'll come up with it later?"

"We can't wait too long," Gideon said. "I'd better see him." He had already decided what to do with Cox today. "Get him on the line for me, will you?" He glanced through other reports as Bell called Cox's office. Abbott was waiting for an interview. There were several other jobs on which the men in charge needed briefing; an hour altogether. "Make it eleven o'clock," Gideon called across, and Bell wiggled a finger. Then he said:

"When you find him, ask him to come along to Mr. Gideon's office at eleven o'clock, will you?"

Abbott had nothing new to report, but his new mood and determination reported itself. Gideon decided to let him defer an announcement of the finding of Marjorie Belman's body for another forty-eight hours. It seemed so harmless and so right. Quite unaware of what the decision could mean to the murdered girl's sister, Gideon soon forgot Abbott and Carraway. Parsons came in, a clerical cherub, to report full co-operation from all hotels.

Bell said that all big stores had been asked to draw up special plans for watching for shop-lifters.

London Airport reported that they could not trace the

arrival of anyone named O'Hara. Washington cabled full description and a dossier of O'Hara, adding: *You can expect officers Webron and Donnelly to arrive London early tomorrow Tuesday.*

Glasgow telephoned, to say that Benny Klein had spent the week-end with Jock Gorra, of the Black Boys. Gideon noted this, and also that there was a negative report on Alec Sonnley.

By the time Gideon had been through all of this, given instructions and made suggestions, cabled the negative report to Washington, and glanced through Cox's report again, it was nearly eleven. Big Ben was striking the hour when there was a sharp tap at the door.

"Come in," called Gideon.

Cox was as spruce as any new pin, immaculate in a medium grey suit, handkerchief showing in his breast pocket, tie to match it. He came in with almost military precision, and closed the door smartly.

"Good morning, Commander."

"Take a pew," Gideon invited, exerting himself to be affable. "You've been busy over the week-end, I see." He pushed a black lacquer box of cigarettes across the desk. "Smoke?"

"No, thank you."

Stiff as a board, Gideon thought gloomily. That might not matter much if Cox did his job really well, but it could create the conditions for serious mistakes or omissions.

Cox sat down, and kept silent.

"Can't see any big problems in this," said Gideon. If he congratulated the other it would seem patronizing, and he was sure that would be the wrong tactics. "We'll need to check with the Commissioner and Traffic about blocking off the two bridges, but I think they'll take your advice. Will you check with Traffic?"

"Very well."

"You've asked for a thousand uniformed men to be drafted in from the other divisions. Sure it will be enough?"

"I think so—together with the eight hundred special constables we can call on."

"How many will we want for the days preceding the Procession?" asked Gideon, almost casually.

He sensed on the instant that Cox had in fact overlooked that, and was suddenly acutely aware of the omission. He went pale, and his lips set more tightly. It seemed a long time before he said:

"I understood that you required only the Procession details."

"Until we know what men we want before and after, we can't tell how many we'll have to spare on the day itself," Gideon said reasonably. "We might need to draft some in from the County forces, and they always want a lot of notice." When Cox didn't respond, he went on: "Will you get the total figures out, allow for rest periods, and then let's have a look at the whole picture again?"

"Very well."

"Thanks," said Gideon, and now his manner was as stiff as Cox's.

When Cox had gone, Bell said caustically: "That's what comes from putting jumped-up louts in big positions."

It wasn't often that Bell sounded bitter about his comparatively low rank, and Gideon let the remark pass. It was half past eleven. He wanted to check a lot of things with Rogerson before lunch so that he could go out and see some of the London Divisions. Each one would have its problems for the Visit, and he knew from experience that if he went to see each Division on its own ground he could get a better view of the situation.

There was little time to worry too much about Cox.

Cox left Gideon's office pale-faced and hard-eyed. He knew that Gideon had had to make his point, but in his highly sensitive mood, Cox told himself that Gideon had talked to him as if to a junior official, had given him "orders".

He hadn't said a word about the perfection of detail of

the proposals, but took that for granted; his only interest seemed to be in finding fault.

Just before twelve noon Gideon went along to Roger-son's office, gave a perfunctory knock, and strode in. Miss Timson was sitting at her desk, with a typewriter in front of her. There was no mistaking the impatience with which she looked at him above the paper in the machine.

"Mr. Rogerson in?" demanded Gideon.

"No," said Miss Timson.

"Where is he?"

"I don't know."

Gideon said: "Well, find out and let me know, and be quick about it." He went out, and the door slipped from his grip as he closed it, and slammed. He was annoyed with himself the moment he heard it bang, still annoyed when he got back to his office. There was no need to behave as Cox wanted to. As he opened the door, one of the telephones on his desk rang, and Bell started to get out of his chair. "I'll take it," said Gideon. He lifted the receiver and growled: "Gideon."

"This is the Assistant Commissioner's Deputy Secretary," announced Miss Timson. "I would like to speak to Commander Gideon."

No "please".

"Speaking," Gideon said.

"I have ascertained that Colonel Rogerson is confined to his bed with a temperature, Commander, and is not likely to be in the office for three days," said Miss Timson. "I am instructed to give you all the assistance you may require."

Gideon managed to say quite mildly: "Thanks. Have you made a start on the hotel arrangements for the French security men?"

"Arrangements have been finalized, Commander. Some men will stay at the Embassy, most at hotels. All the German officials will stay at the Embassy, so will the American security men who come with the President, but the two men coming in advance wish to stay at a hotel."

Gideon found himself smiling.

"Thanks," he said. "Fix up for those two American security officers for tomorrow. Better have about four double bedrooms in reserve, too, or eight singles. We might get others who don't want to stay at the embassies. Have you got access to the Assistant Commissioner's files for the last State Visit?"

"They are in front of me."

"Familiarize yourself with all arrangements," Gideon instructed. "And for the Procession itself, arrange fifty places at least to be available for our senior officers and members of their families at the Ministry building on the corner of Whitehall and Parliament Square."

"Very well, Commander."

"Also in the file you'll find details of what help we received from the Divisions—number of men in uniform, number of C.I.D. personnel, number of women police constables. Have details for each Division tele-typed to every Division, marked provisional. Let me have several copies with good margins for notes and alterations, and let Mr. Cox of Uniform have three copies."

"Very good."

"Get what help you need from the typing pool."

"Very well."

"Report to me when it's all done, will you?" Gideon rang off, and Bell grinned across. "That'll keep her out of mischief for a while! Joe, I'm going over to N.E., and then I want to double back to K.L. Tell them I'm on the way."

"I'll warn 'em," promised Bell.

Gideon went out of the office and down the stairs as Big Ben struck twelve. The sun was breaking through heavy cloud again, and striking hot. Traffic was fairly heavy, with a great deal of truck and trailer movement heading for Lambeth Bridge, and for the New Kent Road, when he reached Blackfriars. He took a short cut towards Billingsgate, passing out of his own area into the district covered by the City of London Police. Once through the traffic at the London Bridge bottleneck, he was able to move faster, for the day's market sales were nearly finished. A few lorries were still being loaded with huge, slimy-looking boxes all marked *Grimsby*, and the stink of fish was very high.

The cobbles on Tower Hill were fairly clear, although soon there would be the throng of office workers eating out, the usual orators on the spot where the gibbet had once stood. It was hard to realize that festive crowds had gathered with their oranges and apples, their knitting and their scandal sheets and ballads of condemned men, to watch the public hangings. Where today political speakers droned, the tumbrils had passed only a hundred and fifty years ago. The grey mass of the Tower of London gave the curious impression that it had been built last year, the stone was so clean. Beefeaters in red and black uniforms were answering questions at the gates, some youths in battle-dress trousers and shirts were kicking a football about in a moat which had once been the Tower's shield against enemies from the rest of London and the surrounding countryside.

Gideon drove past the Mint, reflecting that hordes of people would come here during the Visit; he must soon have a word with the City Police, who would be in charge here.

He turned into Aldgate, where London seemed suddenly to become a working-class suburb, where traffic was moving at a crawl, diesel fumes were stinking, motors had a sullen note. He worked his way round the mean streets to N.E. Divisional Police Headquarters, and it was a quarter to one when he entered Christy's office.

Hugh Christy was fairly new at N.E. Division, which was the toughest in London. He was in his middle-forties, military in appearance and manner, brisk in movement and in speech, with rather a big head, and a manner which often seemed aggressive. Bighead was the nickname most often applied to him at the Yard and in his own Division, but it was no longer as harsh and censorious.

Christy had proved in two years that he was able and shrewd.

As he shook hands, and showed Gideon a chair, all in one movement, he said :

"I've got a couple of big steaks on order. They're ready to go under the grill when I press the button."

"Suits me fine," said Gideon.

Christy's finger prodded a bell-push, twice. Then he squared his shoulders and sat very erect behind his flat-topped desk. "They'll come in and get the table ready ten minutes before we start to eat. Any complaints, George?"

"Lot of worry," replied Gideon mildly. "I'll need all the men you can spare, uniformed and C.I.D., for the big show, and a lot of spade-work between now and then."

"As per memo," said Christy.

"What memo?"

"Yours."

"I haven't sent round any memo yet."

"Came through on the teletype ten minutes ago—here it is," said Christy. He pushed a sheet of foolscap-sized paper across the desk, and Gideon saw the instructions for the Divisions exactly as he had told Miss Timson to send them. Beneath his amusement was annoyance, even resentment. "Don't tell me your memory's slipping," Christy quipped.

"No," said Gideon. In fact, Miss Timson was simply setting out to prove her efficiency, like Cox. "I'm using a secretary who keeps beating the gun."

"Pleasant change to have a quick one," said Christy. "Any special angles?"

"I'm told that Benny Klein, Alec Sonnley's right-hand man, is away."

"That's right. He went off north with the blonde he's living with, and didn't tell anyone where he was going. But I know the mob he works with," said Christy. Then he began to frown, and rubbed the bridge of his nose. "Come to think, a lot of them have gone off on holiday. I noticed that earlier in the week, and didn't think anything of it, just thought they were taking advantage of the weather. Think Sonny Boy Sonnley is preparing for the big show?"

"Probably."

"I'll keep an eye on him," promised Christy grimly. "Don't you worry."

"How many shops has Sonny Boy got in your manor?"

"Three."

"Concentrate on them," said Gideon. "I'll have all his other shops closely watched, too. With luck, we'll get him on this job. But don't have any of Sonnley's or Klein's boys followed unless Lemaitre asks you to. He's gone to find out where Klein's been."

"Everyone on the ball," Christy approved.

"Did you get a memo from Rip, before he left?"

"Yes, and we're watching for French and Muslim Algerians and known agitators."

Gideon was satisfied that nothing would be missed in N.E. Division, and after a good lunch he made two telephone calls to Superintendents of Divisions on the perimeter of the Metropolitan area. He left the N.E. station at ten past two, and drove straight to K.L., where Superintendent Jackson was in charge, the district where Alec Sonnley and Bruce Carraway lived. Four of Carraway's five garages and showrooms were in this area.

Jackson, big, blond and bluff, had received his memo by teleprinter, and everything was in hand. From his office, Gideon telephoned the Yard.

"Joe," he said to Bell, "tell Timson to prepare a memo asking for a special check on all goods sold from Sonnley's shops and warehouses during the three days of the Visit. And tell her without comment not to send it off until I've seen it."

"So you've picked up that teleprint notice she sent out."

"Yes."

"You ought to talk to that woman," said Bell.

"When the time comes," promised Gideon. "Anything new in?"

"Abbott wants to release the identification of Marjorie Belman to the Press. He plans to have Carraway, Little and Atkinson trailed all today, and break the news in the papers tomorrow morning. He thinks that one would be bound to crack."

"Tell him I'll talk to him this evening."

"Right," said Bell. "By the way, that telephoto of O'Hara's in. I've sent it over to Special Branch, and they're going to check with the Airport right away. He's a pretty nondescript type."

"Pity," grunted Gideon. "Get copies round to the Divisions, will you?"

Later, Gideon drove past the big, flashy looking garage slowly, and saw Little talking to a small man by the side of a big American car; there was no sign of Carraway.

A few minutes after the customer interested in the American car had gone, a girl from the office called Little to the telephone. He wiped the palms of his hands as he went to take the call. Every time the bell rang for him he thought it was Beryl Belman, but she hadn't called yet. Had she changed her mind? If she knew he had been at Jorrie's flat, would she go to the police?

"Eric Little speaking," he said.

"You know who this is, don't you?" It was Beryl, with her clear, slightly Cockney voice. "I hope you've got some news for me, Mister Little."

"Yes, I have," said Little eagerly. "You needn't worry, I've got plenty. Meet me tonight, at the Pond, at nine o'clock . . ."

Marjorie Belman was dead. Beryl Belman was walking with death. Other people were unaware of it, but were also moving towards danger. Two of these were in grave danger indeed: a girl of seventeen named Doris Green, who lived in Whitby, and a middle-aged man, named Arthur Ritter, who lived in Worcester.

Both planned, that very day, to come to London for the Visit. They did not know of each other's existence. The girl had decided to come as cheaply as possible, by motor coach ; the man intended to come by train, first class, and to hire a car in London.

Grace Smith was in the shadows, too — like everyone who would be near the spot when her husband threw his bomb.

13

CLOSING SHADOWS

"He'd better come tonight," Beryl said to herself. "If he doesn't, I'm not going to be put off any longer. I'm going straight to Carraway."

It was dark near the Pond, and there were fewer people about tonight. Two men with dogs on leashes were standing together and talking, not far away, and the dogs were sniffing at each other. Cars passed slowly, engines whispering. It was a quiet, balmy night, and even footsteps disturbed the stillness. An owl screeched from the trees in a garden nearby.

"He'd *better* come," Beryl repeated.

She did not really know what to do if Eric Little failed her again. The week-end had been one long worry, for the more she had thought of Carraway, and his effect on Little, the more scared she had become. On the other hand, her mother was listless and sick, her father irritable, and there was little doubt that it would take them a long time to recover—unless Jorrie came back soon.

But suppose Jorrie did have a baby?

"She couldn't have!" Beryl exclaimed, *sotto voce*. "She couldn't have been such a fool. She would know how to make sure she was all right."

Then Beryl thought : *Would she?*

A car turned off the road and drew fairly close to her. She stared at it ; this had *better* be Little. It was a quarter past nine already, and if he was standing her up, she would let him know all about it. The absurdity of the thought passed her by.

The car crawled closer.

It might be someone trying a pick-up, Beryl reminded herself ; men were all the same, the beasts. If it was, she would give him a piece of her mind. Her heart beat fast as the car drew nearer; it was an old Austin, not the kind of car she would expect Little to drive. If this was some old beast—

"Beryl?" a man whispered.

It was Little!

She went forward quickly, as the car slowed down, and at last she recognized him. He sat rather far back in his seat, away from the window, but she was so pleased that he had come that she did not notice anything peculiar about this. She believed that her sister was alive, and still had no reason at all to suspect the awful danger which was closing in on her.

"Yes, I'm here." She sounded eager.

"Hop in," said Little. He leaned farther away from her and opened the far door; to get in she had to go round the other side, but she did not worry about that. In a few seconds she was sitting by his side, and almost before the door had closed, the car was moving off. She sensed his nervousness, and looked round.

"What are you looking round for?" Little demanded harshly.

"Well, I—"

"Has someone been following you?"

"No, of course not. I—I thought *you* were scared. Is Carraway— ?" she broke off.

"No need to worry about Carraway tonight," said Little, in a lower voice. "I'll look after that swine in future, don't you worry."

Beryl sat absolutely still, her hands in her lap, worried by the venom in this man's voice and by the implication in what he said. She was almost too nervous to ask questions. He drove more quickly once he was away from the Pond, heading for the Heath itself. She saw the lights from distant houses and the far-off streets. It was true that she did not know the Heath well, but she was aware that it was a big stretch of common land, several miles across, that roads led over it, and that in places it was unlit and eerie. On Bank Holidays the whole place became alive and alight with all the fun of the fair. She had twice been here for a night of furious excitement, but now the dipped headlights of Little's car seemed hardly to make any impression on the darkness.

Yet she was thinking mostly about Jorrie.

"What—what have you found out?" she made herself ask at last.

"Found out?"

"About—about Jorrie."

"Oh, *Jorrie*!" His manner was peculiar, and she could not understand it, but she was not yet frightened. "Well, Carraway turned her out—that's what the swine did. He let her down flat. Got tired of her, and turned her out."

Beryl gasped: "No!"

"Yes, he did. Boasted about it, too—I made him talk to me this afternoon," Little went on. He spoke as if he were under the stress of some great emotion, but there was nothing to tell Beryl that it was the outward manifestation of his intention to kill. He was talking just to keep her quiet until they reached the spot where he planned to kill her. He knew it well; it was just off the road, hidden by shrubs and trees, exactly where he had once strangled another girl because she might break up his family life. "I told you he was a swine, didn't I?" he went on.

"But—where *is* Jorrie?" When Little didn't answer, fear clutched at Beryl like a cold hand at her heart. "Where is she? She's all right, isn't she? She didn't—she didn't *do* anything to herself?"

Little shot a glance at her as they passed beneath one of the last lamps.

"No," he said, "—she's okay."

"Are you sure?"

"Yes, she's okay."

"Where is she?"

"She's—well, there's a little place on the Heath, that's where she is."

"A place?"

"Little house," he said. His voice seemed to be getting

hoarse. "Over on the heath—she's staying there with a friend. That's where we're going."

"Is she all *right* ?" repeated Beryl shrilly.

"I tell you she's okay," Little said sharply. "Stop worrying. I'm taking you to her, aren't I ?" He turned off the road along a rough track which led to a copse and to shrubs; ahead of them were the stars and in the distance a haze of light over the fringes of Greater London. "Won't be long," he added. He moved his hand to the instrument panel, and something clicked; it was even darker outside, and the lights did not seem to be working at all. For the first time, a twinge of fear caught Beryl, but she took no notice of it. She did not know that they were moving along in darkness, now, and could not be seen from the road.

"How—how far is it ?"

"Just over there," Little said. His voice had become hoarse. His emotion or excitement seemed to be getting greater. "Don't you worry, I know where it is." He turned the wheel of the car and then slowed down; and the next moment, he stopped.

It was a moment of sudden dread for Beryl Belman.

In that instant she realized that there was no house near by, that they were here in darkness, remote from other people; she was alone with this man. She heard him breathing hard. She had read about men like him; sex maniacs, that's what they called them, sex maniacs. She sensed the truth in a tiny flash of time, as his hands left the wheel.

"What— ?" she began.

She felt his hands against her, one thrusting hard across her breast without lingering, the other scraping across her shoulders. Next she felt pressure at the back of her neck and at the front, the awful pressure of this man's hands. Outside there was blackness; inside, the dark horror, and his gasping breath, and those fingers, squeezing with savage strength, as if he couldn't wait to choke the life out of her.

She believed she was going to die.

She felt an awful explosion of terror and pain as if her

very heart was splitting. She heard herself gasping for breath in great hawking noises which drowned those of the man's heavy breathing, noises which seemed to get louder and louder and to be inside her head. She could not struggle. He had trapped her so that she could not move. There was tightness round her chest, becoming closer and closer, and pain like a stabbing knife.

Then, suddenly, the nightmare vanished. Lights blazed, men shouted, Little squealed, the doors opened. Half conscious, Beryl was aware of moving figures, of heads and shoulders blotting out the stars, of Little being dragged out, of a man putting an arm round her shoulder, and speaking with a kind of gentle urgency :

"It's all right, don't worry. You'll be all right."

That was the first time for a week that she had forgotten her sister.

"I thought I'd better call you at home," Abbott said into Gideon's telephone just before midnight. "I thought you'd like to know that we got one swine, even if we haven't got Carraway yet. The worst thing about it is what nearly happened to the sister." Abbott was talking very fast, and Gideon did not attempt to stop him. "If I'd released the news of the murder earlier, it would never have happened. That's what worries me. Hell of an experience the kid had. She'll be all right, though. I've talked to the hospital doctor. Shock and bruising, that's about all—she should be all right in a couple of days."

"That's good," said Gideon, at last. "That's fine."

"Damn lucky we had Little shadowed. If it hadn't been for you I would have concentrated on Carraway," said Abbott. "Don't know, though, after I knew that Little wore a ring . . . It was Little who went off with the other sister, from Piccadilly . . ."

Abbott told the story in the next five minutes, gradually getting more order into his mind and into his sentences. He would be bitterly angry with himself because his tactics had turned sour on him, and it was no use Gideon saying that he was at least as much to blame. That was the worst part about his job; the consequence of failure, or of doing the wrong thing.

The consequences, for instance, that would follow any failure over the Visit.

". . . well, good night, George. Oh, I meant to tell you, I've seen the Belman parents. They're badly cut up, but they've got some neighbours in. They'll be all right. It's been quite a night."

"I bet it has," said Gideon. "What's Little's wife like?"

Abbott said, as if surprised: "Didn't I tell you? She looked struck dumb. She did really, George—struck dumb. The only time I felt sorry for Little was when he kept crying out about his wife, begging me not to tell her until the morning, to let her have a good night's sleep. He's got triplets, aged seven, you know. Two girls and a boy."

Gideon rang off, but stood by the telephone for a few minutes, letting the whole story run through his mind, relieved because of what had been avoided, glad that one case was partly solved, although there was as yet no proof that Carraway was involved. This strange oblivion was at once the frightening and the compelling factor in his life: this complete unawareness of what evil other people were doing and planning.

Was *anyone* planning trouble for the Visit?

In Glasgow, Benny Klein was experimenting with a little water pistol, using corrosive acid instead of water in the rubber holder. Tomorrow morning he would know how the rubber stood up to the acid. If it burned through, he would have to think of something else. Jock Gorra was watching—staring—fascinated.

A little farther south, and on the east coast of England, little Dorris Green, a pretty girl who worked in a coal order office, lay in her single bed, lonely and yet happy. She was deciding what clothes she would take with her to London for the holiday she longed for.

And in a London suburb, Matthew Smith was dreaming of throwing a bomb into the air—a bomb meant to kill one man, but which could also kill dozens or might injure hundreds in or near the big new stand.

In that strange, half-realized world of the mind, Gideon was aware of such dangers as these, and felt helpless because of them. He lay wide awake, next to Kate, fighting the shadows which the Visit cast over London.

14

INVASION

"Commander," said Miss Timson, early on the Wednesday morning.

"Yes?"

"F.B.I. Agent Webron and Secret Service Agent Donnelly are now due at London Airport at eleven-fifteen this morning, and the latest information is that the flight will be on time. Visibility is good. Superintendent Abbott will be at the airport in connection with the Carraway investigation, making arrangements for a watch on all passengers answering the descriptions of Carraway or any of his salesmen. So I have asked him to meet Lieutenant Webron and Mr. Donnelly. Accommodation has been booked for them at the Piccadilly Hotel, which is very central. Have you any further instructions?"

"What time are they due at the hotel?"

"There should be no delay at the customs shed," said Miss Timson. "I imagine that they will be at the hotel at twelve noon."

"Be there to meet them," ordered Gideon. "Have lunch with them and bring them over here for two-thirty."

Miss Timson seemed too startled to respond.

"Good-bye," said Gideon, and rang off. Bell was leaning back in his chair, pencil poised, shaking his head slowly.

"You crafty old so-and-so."

"No woman as efficient as our Miss Timson can be bitchy all the time," said Gideon. "Anything in about O'Hara?"

"Not a thing," replied Bell. "No one at the airport can say for sure that a man answering his description came in this week."

"Did you get plenty of prints of his photograph done?"

"A hundred and fifty."

"That's enough. Send one to each Divisional station and sub-station, with an instruction to report to me if the man's seen."

Bell nodded, but before he spoke, Gideon's telephone rang again, and he lifted the receiver : "Gideon."

"I have made a note of your instructions about the reception of the two American security officials," said Miss Timson, in a rather less acrid voice, "but there is another matter, Commander."

"What is it?"

"The usual space allotted to us on the roof and balconies of the Ministry Corner Building will not be available on this occasion, as special requests have been made for extra space by the Foreign Secretary and the Home Secretary for official guests."

"Oh," said Gideon, and thought how disappointed Kate would be. "Well, see what you can do on the route."

"The official accommodation is limited because of repairs being carried out on the façades of other buildings," reported Miss Timson. "However, permission has been granted to Public Utilities Limited to erect a public stand with a thousand seats, at the corner of Old Scotland Yard. I have been in touch with Public Utilities Limited and they are perfectly willing to allot us twelve complimentary seats, and we may have a further twenty at half price."

Gideon said : "Nice of them. We'll have 'em all for emergency use, and remember my wife wants one."

"Very good, Commander."

"That the lot?"

"I am a little puzzled by the use of the term 'Secret Service' to describe the second American, a Mr. Donnelly."

"It's the title they use for the security branch which looks after the President—nothing really secret about it. Webron is from the Federal Bureau of Investigation in

116

Washington, to liaise with the C.I.D. itself. Donnelly's the liaison with Special Branch."

"Thank you," said Miss Timson.

"Right." Gideon rang off, and immediately lifted the receiver again. "Mr. Cox, Uniform," he said, and then in an aside to Bell : "Anything in from Lemaitre?"

"He's going to telephone at eleven o'clock."

"Parsons?"

"He's waiting to see you."

"We haven't detailed anyone to cover Soho yet," remarked Gideon, and then heard Cox say :

"Deputy Commander speaking."

"'Morning," said Gideon, gruffly. "Gideon here. Can you spare me half an hour?"

"Yes, Commander."

"Come over, will you?" asked Gideon.

He rang off, frowning, thinking suddenly of the girl who had so nearly died on Hampstead Heath. It seemed a long time ago, although only yesterday a pale, frightened Little had been remanded for eight days. He had talked wildly about Carraway, but so far there was no real evidence against his employer. "I'll see Parsons," Gideon decided, and was standing up when Parsons came in briskly, face round and chubby. "'Morning," said Gideon. "What's on your mind?"

"Not enough," Parsons declared. "I wondered if—" he paused, deliberately, with that innocent expression which made him so like a rubicund cleric.

"Go on."

"I've got a hundred per cent response from the hotels, so the rest is routine," said Parsons. "And as I'm to be around the West End most of the time, I wondered if you'd like me to try Soho."

"Ho-ho," Bell said, almost inaudibly.

"Why?" asked Gideon.

"For the strip-clubs and the gambling clubs, the whore-shops and the innocents," answered Parsons. Gideon had never known a man more sure of himself. "Bound to get a lot of out-of-town visitors. London wouldn't be London 'without its haunts of vice. But we ought to have the clubs watched for con-men, and . . ."

There was a tap at the door.

"Come in," Gideon called, and Cox entered with his now familiar precision. He looked startled at sight of Parsons, but closed the door and came forward. " 'Morning, Mr. Cox," said Gideon, formally. "Do you know Superintendent Parsons?"

"We have met," Cox said.

"Several times," said Parsons.

"Good. Superintendent Parsons is going to be in charge of the watch on the hotels, the clubs, strip-clubs and disorderly houses," explained Gideon. "I think it would help if he sat in on this discussion."

"Yes," said Cox.

"Of course," Parsons said, but looked puzzled.

"Any luck with those estimates of men required?" Gideon asked, and Cox handed him a file. "Thanks." Gideon opened the folder, spread it out on his desk, then spread out a similar list of men required from the C.I.D., said : "Pull your chairs round," and began to check.

He was completely objective, and gradually Cox thawed. They checked the men required at the various points, with special concentration at the airport, the embassies and hotels, as well as the Procession route. Parsons made occasional succinct suggestions. Gideon made notes about men required at the check-points in eight-hour shifts. Gradually a comprehensive picture was formed.

After an hour, Gideon said : "We need three hundred men more than we've got, each day, and five hundred more on the Procession day."

"Have to work on overtime." Parsons placed the tips of his fingers together.

"I've allowed for two hours' overtime for each of my men," said Cox.

"Good idea. I haven't for mine," Gideon said. He looked across at Bell. "Fix it, Joe, will you?" Before Bell answered, a telephone rang on Gideon's desk, and he picked up the receiver. "Gideon."

It was Lemaitre, calling from Liverpool; he sounded brisk and bright.

"Having a nice quiet time down there, George?" he inquired. "That's good. While I think of it, save Soho for me. That's my beat when I get back."

"It's sold," Gideon said.

"Lecherous old devil," jeered Lemaitre. "But I can't stay here talking . . . I've done Glasgow, Manchester and Liverpool, already. None of the top coppers has heard of any exodus for the Visit; all the local boys seem to have decided to stay at home."

"Any idea why?"

"Benny Klein's left Glasgow, and seen a lot of the mob leaders," answered Lemaitre. "There have been two squeaks. Benny's paying each leader five hundred quid to keep his boys at home, and threatened to use razor and coshboys if they don't. It's a wicked shame, George—Sonny Boy's trying to establish a monopoly."

In spite of himself, Gideon laughed.

"So Sonnley and Klein want the field to themselves."

"Looks like it."

"Any word from Birmingham or Bristol?"

"No one gave me any wings."

"Hire some," urged Gideon. "Okay, Lem. That the lot?"

"Picked up a funny little thing," said Lemaitre.

"How funny?"

"Some of the car hire firms up in these wild parts are getting letters from Carraway, offering to take orders for cars for hire in London during the Visit."

"Cheap?"

"Not on your life! Double the usual price. That's how it was found out—one of the Glasgow chaps moaned about it to a pal of his in the Force."

"So it's business as usual with Carraway," Gideon mused. "Thanks, Lem, that might come in useful." He rang off, and after a moment looked across at Bell, and went on: "Get the drift of that, Joe?"

"Yes."

"Send another chit out to all our Divisions for a special watch on Klein's boys, and on Sonnley's shops."

"Right."

"Looks as if we're going to have the crooks in our own back yard to worry about," remarked Parsons. "Not many strangers."

"Could be a good thing. You could help us a lot there, Cox," Gideon went on. "Will you brief your chaps to keep a special watch on—"

"Klein, Sonnley, and Company?"

"Yes."

"I will."

"Ta. Now, let's go over the day of the Procession again, shall we? First, lining the route." That job took twenty minutes. "Now, the cordons." That took ten. "Barriers next," said Gideon.

Bell, looking across at the three men, wondered whether Cox and Parsons realized that they were having an object lesson in the power of concentration, plus wide experience, plus an inexhaustible knowledge of London's pomp and circumstance. Gideon said just what was necessary, co-related facts and situations, and did sums in his head by some kind of arithmetical shorthand. He did not let up until, at half past twelve, he leaned back and said :

"Now, all we've got left is the big Public Utilities stand." He got up, and went to a big wall map which had been brought up from the Map Room only that morning. "Come and have a look," he urged, and Cox and Parsons joined him.

He found the spot on the map, and made a red line at the street on the east side of Whitehall, nearly opposite the Horse Guards sentries. His red mark showed exactly where the big temporary stand, of the kind erected for all great occasions, was to be. He showed how this would block the view of some Ministry windows from the street, but these could be covered from the roofs of buildings opposite. No man-holes—the other main source of danger, where an assassin could hide—were hidden. It was safely away from the danger spot where the procession would have to slow down; by the time it arrived here, it would be going at a normal pace. Moreover, allowing only a limited number of spectators to stand in front of the stand, the area would not be too crowded; the essential thing was to keep enough space for free police movement in case of emergency. He did not think of bomb-throwing.

"Make a note not to allow spectators more than two deep in front of the P.U. stand, will you?" he asked.

"Yes," Cox promised.

"And that's about all," Gideon said. "Hope I haven't kept you too long. Wish we could have lunch, but I've got to go down and see those French and German chaps." Gideon fastened his collar, shrugged his coat into position, and smiled at Cox. "Any bright ideas about getting those extra men will be welcome," he said.

"Commander," said Parsons.

"Yes?"

"You forgot Soho."

"You have another look," said Gideon. "Cox's allowed for an extra thirty uniformed men to be around, and we'll need as many from the C.I.D. Will you two work together on this?"

"Sure," said Parsons.

"Very well," said Cox.

Gideon nodded, and went out. He left a silent office behind him, until Parsons held his hands up in a mock gesture of surrender, and said:

"Human atomic power in action. Ever seen anything like it?"

"There isn't anything like it," said Bell.

"*Very* impressive," contributed Cox. It wasn't exactly a sneer, but it certainly wasn't a reflection of the other's mood. "I've one or two urgent jobs, Mr. Parsons. Can we meet after lunch?"

After a pause, Parsons said: "Two-thirty?"

"If you'll come to my office."

"Okay," agreed Parsons. He waited until Cox had gone, then turned round, looked at Bell and let out a long, slow breath.

"Who put his nose out of joint?"

"I give him two more days before Gee-Gee explodes," Bell said.

Cox, hurrying along to his office, was staring straight ahead. He felt as if he had been out in a heavy storm, which had taken all the strength out of him. He was anxious to make notes, copious notes, so as to be sure he missed nothing.

In a peculiar way, Gideon scared him.

Gideon went along to the lift, and downstairs to the larger of the Yard's two cinemas, later than he had meant to be, and with much more to think about than Cox. In the cinema, there were seats for a hundred men, an 8-mm. and a 16-mm. movie projector, and a projector for 35-mm. stills.

The room was only half-filled, with the French security mission in the centre block of seats, the Yard men who would be liaising with them around the perimeter, and four German officers by themselves at the back. A senior from the Uniformed Branch was present; so was Ripple's deputy. The German security officers had come over from Berlin after Ripple's visit. Gideon wished that the two Americans were here, but their plane had been delayed, after all, although arrangements for this session had been left to the last minute. Gideon felt the gaze of nearly every one of the Frenchmen as he took up a position at the screen end of the theatre. Mollet, the man in charge of the French mission, came and joined him.

"Gentlemen," said Gideon, in passable French. "I am very glad to welcome you to London, and I regret only that the average Englishman's French is so poor. Consequently I shall have to speak mostly in English, and so will our chief lecturer. I hope you'll forgive us."

There was a dutiful laugh.

"I don't believe there is one of you who doesn't understand and speak English well," said Gideon. "Is there?" He looked round the men, noticing the difference in the cut of their clothes and the cut of their hair ; hardly one of the Frenchmen could be mistaken for an Englishman, and *vice versa*. "Thanks. I suggest that you sit one and one— one overseas officer next to one English. If there are any points of clarification needed, it will be easier." He waited for the men to shift positions, and Mollet, a grey-haired, smooth-faced man in his fifties, with a drooping mouth and rather heavy-lidded eyes, nodded approval.

"What we're going to do," said Gideon, "is flash on to the screen in the 35-mm. pictures some enlarged maps of the routes from the airport to London, and also of all the other official journeys, as well as the State Procession. We shall explain the normal precautions taken, and the special precautions planned for the State Procession, when all Heads of States will be vulnerable at the same time. The State Procession route will be marked into sections, and after that each section will be shown separately, and on a much larger scale. All understood ?"

There were murmurs of agreement.

"In front of every seat is a booklet showing these same maps, and at the end of the session you will be able to make notes of anything you want to discuss at another meeting. After we have studied the maps on the screen, we shall see two moving pictures of earlier processions. Here you will see not only the places where the crowds are thickest, but how the Metropolitan Police and different regiments of the Army, Navy and Air Force, line the route, making a break through by an individual from the crowds difficult if not impossible. We will then show the moving pictures in slow motion. The whole procedure this afternoon will take about two hours, after we shall break up for half an hour for that peculiarly English institution, afternoon tea. After tea, preliminary questions will be asked and answered. Is that all understood."

There was a chorus of agreement.

"Right," said Gideon. "Let's go." He signalled to the operator, then went down to a front seat, with Mollet, to see the whole thing through.

There were a dozen questions afterwards, and it was Bayer, one of the Germans, who asked the last.

"The stand for spectators, Herr Commander—how will that be guarded?"

"We will have seats on the middle gangway of every fourth row," Gideon answered, and after a moment a diagram of the proposed stand was flashed on to the screen. He pointed to small pencilled numerals which showed in outline. "Here—here—here." He stabbed at a dozen figures. "Then at the side gangways we shall have four men—oné at each side of the top of the stand, another at the bottom. We shall have men at the one entrance—there will only be one entrance although there is the emergency exit. A diagram like this is included in the book in front of you."

"Thank you, Herr Commander," said the German. "I ask one more question?"

"As many as you like."

"Is it possible for each nation, the French, the Americans and we ourselves, the Germans, to be represented in this stand, as well as in the streets?"

"Yes. Are you worried about the stand?"

"A little, Herr Commander," the German said, and sat down. They were all worried, of course.

Gideon left the theatre ahead of the others, went back to his office, and found Bell anxious to see him. Webron and Donnelly had been in, and gone off almost at once; there was a rumour that a man answering O'Hara's description had been seen in a hotel in the Strand.

"And they've gone to watch," Bell said. "They've taken all the files we had for them, to study at the hotel."

"So they're bang on the ball," Gideon remarked.

"They're on the ball all right," Bell said. "I've sent Chann over with them. He'll phone if they have any luck."

At half past six, when Gideon left the office, no word had come through, and the two Americans were still at the hotel in the Strand.

In fact, the man O'Hara was in a private hotel, a kind of glorified boarding-house, in Kensington. He was officially here on vacation, spent a lot of time out of doors with his movie camera, and was no trouble to anybody. That afternoon, while the two men from Washington were on the false trail, O'Hara, who had a passport under the name of Hann, was putting a new magazine of film into his 16-mm. movie camera. At least, that was what it looked like. The magazine of film was in fact a ·22 automatic pistol, operated by the press-button of the camera. O'Hara *alias* Hann practised putting it in every day, so that it would give him no trouble when the right moment came.

O'Hara did more than practise; he prayed.

He was nondescript only in appearance; emotionally he was a man of tremendous power and conviction, and he was convinced, within the narrow limits of his religious bigotry, that Roman Catholicism was an evil thing. During the election campaign he had preached this gospel, fighting desperately against the more liberal-minded, and when the President had been elected on a desperately narrow margin, bitterness had turned to hatred.

O'Hara was a kindly man by nature, a good man by training and conviction, but deeply rooted in him was the belief that men of dark skin were inferior to men of white skin. He had no doubts about this in his own mind, just as he had none about the wrongness of Roman Catholicism.

Then the new President had acted—as well as preached—to give full rights to Negroes. O'Hara, already poised on the delicate balance between religious fervour and religious mania, began to pray and plan for the death of the President.

He knew what would happen to him if he succeeded, and did not care. He believed that he had been privileged by the Almighty to strike the fateful blow.

As the moment drew nearer, his prayers grew more fervent and his handling of the camera-gun more skilful.

"Now we've got to get a move on with this job," said Reggie Simpson, managing director and chief shareholder in Public Utilities and Car Parks. It was the same afternoon, and getting late. "The stand had got to meet the usual London County Council specifications, and if you think you can get away with anything on that, you're making the mistake of your life, chums." He was talking with two foremen who would be in charge of the erection of the stands. "I've worked out the quantity of tubular scaffolding we need, the unions, the boards, the stairs, and the coconut matting. We want twenty men on the job by Monday morning, that's the earliest we can start. Gives us just time to get the job done."

"It'll be a cakewalk," one foreman said.

"When I see it sold out, I'll tell you whether it will be a cakewalk," said Simpson. He was small, perky, and thin-faced, and his Cockney voice could hardly be more nasal. "If you get it done by Saturday night without overtime for the men, there'll be a fifty-quid bonus for each of you. It's blue ruin if the men have to work on Sunday."

"It'll be finished Saturday week," the "cakewalk" foreman assured him.

"Rosie, ducks," said Alec Sonnley when he went in to his evening meal that day, "I've got a little present for you."

"What is it, Sonny?" asked Rosie, mildly. "It won't take too long just now, will it? I've got a pheasant in the oven, and if I don't go and look at it, it'll be overdone, and I know you don't like that."

"And game chips and peas?"

"Yes, dear."

"Okay, then," said Alec Sonnley. "There's a stand going up at the corner of Old Scotland Yard and Whitehall. I've got two of the best seats for you, bang in the front row!"

Rosie's eyes lit up, and her husband was fully satisfied. At that time he had not the slightest inkling of Klein's experiments with corrosive acid.

"Of course we're going to buy the seat," said Gideon. "If I start getting free seats and using them for my family there'll be a screech about corruption the first time anyone hears. You worry too much about money."

"I must admit that I've always wanted to see a big procession," said Kate.

Michael Lumati, reading in the evening paper that Wednesday of the stands which would be available, wondered whether he would treat himself to a good seat, or whether he would stand in the crowd. London's ceremonial occasions had been part of his life since he could remember, and he was looking forward to this particular show for its own sake, as well as for the great opportunity it would give him.

Lumati was sitting pretty with fifteen thousand pounds of near-perfect currency notes, and still his only worry was how to get them distributed.

What he needed, he had to admit, was someone with a lot of shops, or a lot of barrows, and someone with a big turnover during the Visit. The real truth was that he ought to use Sonnley, who had already ordered artwork for special *Souvenir Programmes* for the occasion.

"Mr. Sonnley, I've got an idea for a special Visit Sovenir Catalogue, and another way of making a bit of quick dough," Lumati said on the telephone. "Could you spare me half an hour? I don't think we ought to talk about it on the telephone."

"Let's have a drink," said Sonnley. He prided himself that he never missed a chance. "How about the Woodcock? You know it?"

He knew quite well that Lumati knew it, and that Lumati was eager for the meeting.

Matthew Smith left his desk in the city, not far from the Tower of London, an hour earlier than usual that day, pleading a headache. There was no specific purpose in his mind. He was on edge, and concentration was very difficult. He thought of that buried bomb as a miser thought of a hoard of gold.

He resisted a temptation to go and see how the stand was progressing, for he did not want to be seen at his chosen spot too often, and travelled by Underground, before the rush hour crammed Londoners in like placid flies clinging to every available piece of floor or seating space, and had the rare luxury of a seat. On the windows of the train were coldly printed green notices:

CERTAIN STATIONS WILL BE CLOSED BETWEEN MIDNIGHT ON JUNE 1st AND SIX O'CLOCK (P.M.) ON JUNE 2nd, THE OCCASION OF THE STATE VISITS. TIME TABLES WILL BE VARIED DURING THAT SAME PERIOD. EXTRA LATE TRAINS WILL BE RUN.   LONDON TRANSPORT SERVICE

Smith thought: *I'll have to get out at Charing Cross. It makes no difference.*

He kept picturing the Queen's carriage, kept wondering who would come next, kept seeing the picture of the President of France sitting proud and erect in his gilded carriage. He clenched his right hand as if the bomb were in it, and his mind went through the motions of tossing it through the air. He could even picture the scene—the panic, the cries, the rush of people. For some reason he did not see the blood or the smashed faces, and he did not hear the screams of the innocent people there to watch the colourful pageantry.

He had never given a thought to escaping, either, and it did not occur to him now. He simply had to throw that bomb.

There was no sign of Grace at home and he was glad; Grace was intolerable these days, always watching him, always asking if he felt all right. It was almost as if she suspected what was in his mind.

Nonsense!

He put on the kettle for some tea, and while waiting for it to boil was drawn as if by irresistible force towards the workshop in the garden. He smoothed down his hair as he went towards it, more relaxed than he had been for hours.

Then he reached the window, and glanced in.

His wife was on one knee, and bricks were out of the floor at the spot where his bomb was buried.

Grace Smith had never been so worried in her life.

She was sure that something serious was the matter with Matthew; she had known it for a long time. She feared for his mind. Ever since the death of their son there had been moments, sometimes whole hours, when his eyes had glazed over and an expression of incalculable pain had tightened his features, drawing them up in a kind of contorted mass of nerves—as if he hated.

His eyes had become feverish for days on end, his manner jumpy, he had shouted at her, had sunk into long periods of silence—and spent a lot of time in his workshop. When this strange manifestation had reappeared, she had tried to remember the exact circumstances of the first occasion, and one thing had been easy to recall. It had been on a great day in London, when some big pot from the Continent had visited the Queen. Grace Smith never failed to go and watch the great processions; the displays of England's pageantry fascinated her. For royal weddings, she would wait all night to get a good view of the happy couple—a view lasting twenty or thirty seconds or so.

On the morning when Matthew had turned on her so furiously, Grace Smith had feared the truth with a great and terrible fear.

She had to help Matthew, but she could not allow a terrible thing to happen.

She ought to tell the police . . .

But she might be wrong, she reminded herself; she was only guessing.

It would be a *terrible* thing if Matthew . . .

She had to find out for sure, and it dawned on her that if she did, if she confronted Matthew with her knowledge, it would be enough to deter him. That was the all-important thing. He would need a weapon, a gun or—or even a bomb. The obvious place to hide it was in the workshop.

And there *was* something.

It looked like a small vacuum flask, but was lying in a bed of cotton wool, and the bricks she had discovered loose had cotton wool stuck on them, too. Only a high explosive would be so well protected. She knelt by the side of the little hole, staring down, horrified, terrified.

The she heard a sound, glancing around in alarm, and saw Matthew.

He was coming in. His eyes were staring. His hands were clenched, and held some distance in front of him. Sight of him like this should have terrified her, but in fact it did not. She rose from her knees, and spoke quite calmly.

"Is this a bomb, Matthew?"

He didn't answer.

"Are you planning some terrible crime?" She was still calm.

Matthew stopped two yards away from her, staring, lips parted now, breath hissing through them.

"Matthew, answer me." When he did not answer, she went on as if she were talking to their lost son, in those days when he had been changing from boy to adolescent; when she, not Matthew, had realized there was a bad streak in him. She had always believed that he had killed that French girl, although she had never breathed a word of that to Matthew. "Matthew," she declared, "you're not well. You're not well, I tell you. We've got to go away together, at once. We—"

Then, only then, did she realize her awful danger. A shimmering brightness such as she had never seen made his eyes hideous. His lips twisted, his hands seemed to writhe in front of her.

"Matthew!" he gasped. "Matt—"

He sprang at her, and carried her back against the bench, then got his hands about her throat and squeezed and squeezed.

It was a long, back-breaking task to pull up more bricks, dig a deep hole, put his wife's body in it, then replace the bricks and fill all the cavities between them with dirt. It took almost as long to load a wheelbarrow, after dark, and carry the displaced soil out into the garden.

But the bomb was safe.

15

VICE-MAN

Parsons was a funny chap, thought Gideon. He gave the impression of being a bit flabby in body and mind, a bit too facile with words, everything to all men; but he absorbed work like a sponge, did it quickly and efficiently, and came up smiling, asking for more. He also absorbed knowledge about London's vice spots, and it had been said that he knew every prostitute by name—much as an earnest curate might, when he saw each as a soul to win. There was nothing even slightly sanctimonious about him when he came into Gideon's office at nine o'clock next morning, even though he wore a pre-sermon kind of smile.

"'Morning, skipper."

"What's making you so happy?"

"Just being my natural self," replied Parsons. "Like the Deputy Commander, U.B."

"What's that?"

"He's bending over backwards to be Mr. Efficiency but he's got some bee in his bonnet. None of my business, but—may I go on?"

"Yes."

"He's not sure whether to hate himself or Commander Gideon," said Parsons. "He's got Uniform at his fingertips, though. Joe Bell was saying that he's asking for trouble. I know, so am I. Will you leave Cox to me for a bit?"

There weren't two other men at the Yard who would go this far with Gideon. Gideon stared at the half-smiling face for a long time, before he said:

"Yes."

"Thanks, skipper," said Parsons. "Mucho gracias. I've been over the Soho district with him, and I think everything's laid on. In the big clubs we'll have two men and a woman, and Uniform will have regular quarter-hour street patrols, in pairs. We won't stop the vice that way, but we can stop it from becoming too blatant. I drifted in on the strip-club kings and queens, too."

Gideon was smiling.

"Warned them that we wanted no extravaganzas, no special private exhibitions of sexual peculiarities, a firm bar against all under-ages—they're to keep 'em out—and no doorway soliciting. If they'd play, I said we'd play. Okay?"

"Yes."

"Thanks," Parsons said again. "I gave the gaming houses a miss."

"Why?"

"If we try to cover them, too, we'll be stretched too tight. Better a man lost his bank balance than a boy his virginity."

"Don't let the gamblers know."

"No."

"Anything else?" asked Gideon.

"One thing that wants a bit of deep thought," Parsons answered. "At least a dozen Italian prostitutes have come in during the past week, all very high class. You might think about trying for wholesale extradition orders. They're organized by a man called Sapelli, Luigi Sapelli. He's taken over a couple of houses in Green Street, all one-room apartments."

"We'd never get wholesale extradition," objected Gideon.

Parson's grin was more devil's than Christian.

"Sapelli doesn't know that."

"You want to warn him?"

"Just tell him we don't like vice in London organized by outsiders; we prefer the home product. But I don't think *we* should tell him."

Gideon thought : *Now what's he up to?* and he asked : "Who should?"

"Our native Soho boys," replied Parsons, smoothly.

"A few threats from them would do a lot of good. If Sapelli thinks his ladies aren't going to get many customers, he may send some of them home."

"No," decided Gideon, promptly. "That could lead to a lot of trouble. Is Sapelli from Milan or Rome?"

"Milan."

"Try to get enough on him to extradite him," Gideon said. "Let me know what we're doing, too."

Parsons rubbed his fleshy hands together.

"Okay, skipper," he said. "I'll do just that."

Gideon had a sneaking feeling that "just that" was exactly what Parsons had wanted to do, but had preferred it to come as an order.

Parsons went off, leaving Gideon alone in the office. He put Parsons out of his mind—Parsons could be left to his job all right. Joe Bell was with Miss Timson, sending out reports and instructions. There were two telephone calls from Divisions and five minutes' breather before the operator told him that Lemaitre was on the line, from Birmingham.

"Hallo, Lem."

"You up already?" Lemaitre could seldom resist being facetious. "George," he went on, "there is a fishy smell."

"In Birmingham?"

"No, Glasgow. I got a squeal."

"What is it?" asked Gideon.

"Benny Klein's been here in Birmingham, and talked to all the big boys," Lemaitre announced. "Now he's going back to Glasgow. The word is that the Glasgow group will be in London for the Visit, but the others will stay home."

"You mean Gorra of Glasgow is going to defy Klein?" Gideon could see the inevitable consequences of such an invasion. It would almost certainly lead to warfare between gangs of pickpockets and shop-lifters; it might bring out the razors and the bicycle chains, the coshes and the flick-knives. If that happened, police urgently needed for normal crowd control would have to be diverted, which would create a lot of difficulties.

"That's the fishy smell," Lemaitre told him, sounding really puzzled. "Klein and Jock Gorra are like old buddies."

"Does that mean that Klein's fooled him?"

"I don't know what it means. I just don't like it."

"I'll warn the Divisions," Gideon said. "Lem, while you're on—ask Birmingham if they could spare us a hundred men, say, if their gangs do move out. Just see how the wind blows. If they'll play, I'll get an official request sent up from the Commissioner, but we don't want to ask and be refused."

"Right," said Lemaitre. "I'm going on to Bristol tonight, and should be back on Saturday. Okay?"

"Fine."

"Take care of London for me," Lemaitre quipped, and rang off.

Gideon was pondering over this unexpected and puzzling news from Birmingham when his telephone bell rang. He lifted it, said: "Gideon," gruffly, and heard a man speak in an American accent. From one aspect of London during the Visit, he switched instantly to another.

"Is that Commander Gideon?"

"Yes it is."

"Commander, can you spare me and Agent Donnelly a little time?" It was Webron, of the F.B.I.

"Yes, of course."

"We'll be right along," said Webron, and Gideon rang off. He took out the file on O'Hara, mostly consisting of the dossier which had been brought over from Washington. It was pretty thin. The man had been suspected of plotting against the President, and was known to be a religious bigot—an anti-Catholic. He had made threats against the President soon after the election, and the F.B.I. had discovered that he was an expert in firearms, especially small weapons. There was a note saying: *Ideal for assassinations in crowded places.*

Gideon checked the physical description of O'Hara: five feet seven inches high, sallow complexion, blue-grey eyes, no outstanding feature, no visible distinguishing marks when dressed, although he had an appendectomy scar.

There was a tap at the door.

"Come in," called Gideon, and stood and rounded the desk to greet the Americans.

Webron was short, swarthy, probably Jewish, with thin black hair brushed over his white pate so that it looked streaky; a man with big eyes and a constant half-smile. Donnelly was tall and lean, dressed immaculately, wore his black hair in a crew cut, and wore glasses.

"I've been recapping on O'Hara," Gideon said. "If you could find a single distinguishing facial mark it would help a lot."

"Sure, his looks are as nondescript as they can be," said Webron. He did most of the talking for the pair, and now sat back in an easy-chair, while Donnelly leaned against the mantelpiece. "Commander, we want you to know that we are very satisfied about the efforts you are making, and the precautions you're taking, but we are worried as hell."

"Any particular reason?" Gideon asked.

Webron said: "Yes, there is," and glanced at Donnelly.

"A very good reason," Donnelly said.

"Commander, the Bureau in Washington has dug up more information about O'Hara. They caught an old friend of his, also a good religious hater. This friend says that O'Hara is in England, but that's not all. He says that, before he left, O'Hara perfected an automatic pistol with a fifty-yard range which can be used from a movie camera." After a long pause, Webron added: "How about that?"

Donnelly shifted his position.

"From now on, every time I see a movie camera I'm going to get the shakes," he stated.

Gideon thought bleakly: *So there's real danger.* He looked from one man to the other, and spoke after a long pause: "I'll put more men on to the search. I'll send reminders to all stations. And I'll have reports made on every American or Canadian we can find who has a movie camera. What size is this one?"

"Sixteen millimetre," answered Webron. "And that's some job you're planning."

"It's got to be tried," Gideon said.

When the Americans had gone, he roughed out the order for all London and Home Counties police stations, knowing what a groan would go up when the station chiefs saw it. He sent for Violet Timson, told her to rush it, and then forced himself to read other reports. It wasn't easy at first; it couldn't be done, but he wanted to be out on O'Hara's trail. Soon, however, a report gained his full attention.

Carraway flatly denied everything, and his other salesmen stood by their earlier statements. The truth was that Gideon could not concentrate on Carraway, because problems of the Visit kept obtruding, and he felt a return of the sense of restlessness, the urge to go out and take an active part in a case. He hadn't done much good the last time he'd gone out, but next time—he grinned to himself.

Benny Klein was grinning, too. His sharp-featured sallow face was twisted in an expression of beastly delight as he watched the mouse squirming. It was stuck to a small chromium plated tube which he had smeared with vitriol overnight, and left to dry. Only it hadn't dried; the squeals and antics of the mouse proved that.

Klein sent a postcard to Jock Gorra which read : *"I've got it."*

Fussy Mrs. Benedict, who lived two doors away from the Smiths, wasn't grinning. She was frowning because she was puzzled and a little worried. When her husband came home that evening, he was welcomed with a gusty :

"She still isn't back, Jim. I've been there four times, and there isn't a sign of her. I'm sure if she'd intended to go away she would have told me."

"Oh, you worry too much," said Benedict, a plump, easy-going man, who was already kicking off his shoes. "Matthew Smith is home. I saw him in the garden as I came by. If you're so worried about Grace, why don't you ask him where she's gone?"

"All he'd do is tell me to mind my own business," said Mrs. Benedict.

"I see what you mean," said her husband, solemnly, and glanced out of the window. He saw Matthew Smith locking the door of his workshop before strolling back to the house, but didn't think twice about it.

"I asked my dad, and he said there isn't any need to book a hotel. If you book a place in advance, they'll charge you the earth," said a girl who worked with Doris Green, and envied her the coming visit to London to see the Procession. "He says there are hundreds and hundreds of places in London where you can get bed and breakfast real cheap, but you have to go and seek them out. You've got your money out of the Post Office, haven't you?"

"I took it all out today," Doris told her.

"Well," said the other girl, "take my dad's advice, and don't go throwing any away."

16

COINCIDENCE

GIDEON was in his office at a quarter to eight on Saturday morning, a week later, and Bell was already there. Only the night staff was at the Yard, and Gideon had the usual Saturday morning feeling, that everyone was anxious to get through his job as soon as possible.

A messenger came through with a huge bundle of mail, and envelopes of all shapes and sizes were piled high in front of Bell. He groaned. It was too early for the secretarial staff to be in. Gideon was about to speak when one of his telephone bells rang. He picked up the receiver.

"Gideon."

"Good morning, Commander," said Miss Timson. "I understand that this morning's mail delivery is very heavy."

Gideon had his first relaxed moment so far.

"Mountainous," he said. "If I send it in, will you get it opened?"

"Yes, Commander."

"Eating out of your hand," jeered Bell. "Like to know why our Violet is so chirpy?"

"Why?" asked Gideon, as he rang off.

"She's had a postcard from Ricky Wall, from Berlin," Bell reported. "Couldn't mistake his handwriting, and couldn't mistake the Brandenburg Gate, either."

Gideon said: "Good luck to them. Has Lemaitre been in?"

"No."

"I'm puzzled about that Glasgow business," Gideon said. "Telephone Glasgow and ask for the latest on Jock Gorra, will you? Before I get the post back, I'll go and have a word with Mollet and the German, Bayer. Those two start work at seven every morning. They seem surprised when we don't."

"Who's surprised?" asked Bell. "They sleep all night."

Mollet, the droll-looking Frenchman, and Bayer, big, bullet-headed, almost like a caricature of his race, were proving good friends and good collaborators. They shared an office which had been cleared for them by putting senior Yard men in rooms which were already occupied. They were in fine humour, and Gideon saw their notes, their marked maps, their files, kept in a methodical order which did him good to see. As he turned to go, the door opened, and Webron and Donnelly entered.

"Good morning, Commander. Glad to see you," Donnelly said.

"Everyone is getting here earlier in the morning," Webron remarked. His voice had a trace of mid-European guttural. "Do you consider that a good thing, Commander?"

"Very good indeed," Gideon said. "It allows you plenty of time for sightseeing." He was rewarded with a burst of laughter.

"Anything new in about O'Hara?"

"I'm beginning to wonder if that guy really is in London," Webron said.

Gideon went out, reflecting that for an early morning session it had been remarkably good-humoured. As the door closed, he heard Webron say: "*Gee-Gee's quite a guy.*" Instead of raising Gideon's spirits and keeping them high, that brought about a return of the earlier mood of dissatisfaction with himself.

O'Hara had disappeared among London's millions, adding to general anxiety. The Glasgow situation was a worry. Cox was still an unknown quantity, too. Would it be a good idea to do the rounds with Cox? Or was that simply an excuse to get out of the office? Gideon wondered which job he would go out on, if he could, and unhesitatingly decided that he would join the hunt for O'Hara, who seemed the greatest menace.

A young police constable, named Kemp, strolled past the little private hotel in Kensington, near the High Street, at a time when O'Hara was looking out of the window down into the busy street, and picturing how busy the Procession route would be. O'Hara turned away from the window, went for his camera, brought it forward and trained it on the back of P.C. Kemp. No one saw O'Hara doing it, but had anyone done so it would have looked a perfectly innocent action.

O'Hara, a man in his forties, turned away from the window, sat in a shadowy corner, closed his eyes, and unlocked the camera, then took out the magazine of film, put it in his pocket, took out the other, deadly type of magazine, and placed that into position. His fingers were thin, long, and precise in their movements. When he locked the camera again, he opened his eyes, checked that everything was as it should be, levelled the camera, and pressed the button. The usual whirring sound came, punctuated by little snapping noises: *zpp, zpp, zpp, zpp, zpp, zpp*. Six, in all. When O'Hara put a loaded magazine in, that would mean six bullets.

O'Hara was fully satisfied.

P.C. Kemp went into the Divisional Station for his mid-shift break, and, as always, looked at the noticeboard. A new notice, marked *URGENT*, was pinned up below one about a darts match with Hammersmith.

The notice read :

James Gregory O'HARA—American Citizen
(See Previous Notice)

A report must be made immediately of any American or Canadian or individual speaking with an American or Canadian accent living in this district. If any such person owns a 16-mm. ciné camera this should be reported immediately to the Superintendent's office and in emergency to Commander Gideon at New Scotland Yard.

Particular attention should be given to resi-

141

dents in hotels of all kinds, guest houses, boarding-houses, and apartment houses. The man believed to be O'Hara might be with a party, might be with a woman, or might live on his own.

No risks should be taken with anyone suspected of being O'Hara.

"See that, Dick?" another constable asked. "Got to check every hotel and boarding-house. Wonder what they want him for? Got to have eyes at the back of your head, these days?"

Michael Lumati left his studio on the following Sunday afternoon, took a Number 11 bus to Fulham Broadway, then sauntered towards North End Road, where the litter from the previous night's market had not yet been properly cleared. He turned into a public house, and went upstairs to a private lounge. He could hear a man whistling : *Some Enchanted Evening*. He tapped at the door, the whistling stopped, and Alec Sonnley called :

"That you, Lummy?"

"It's me, Sonny Boy."

"Come right in." Sonnley was standing by a window hung with dark green curtains. An aspidistra stood on a small table in the middle of the room, which was like one preserved as a mid-Victorian relic.

"What are you going to have?" he asked, and turned to a table on which were dozens of bottles of beer.

"I'll have a pale," said Lumati, and sat down in an old-fashioned saddleback armchair as Sonnley poured out.

"Got those samples?" Sonnley asked.

Lumati didn't answer.

"Now listen, Lummy, have you got them or haven't you? If you're still worrying about the busies, forget it— we've got those souvenir programmes to show we're in legitimate business together. But if you're thinking of asking for more than fifty-fifty, forget that, too. I'm taking just as big a risk as you are. You know that as well as I do."

"Yes, I know," said Lumati.

"Don't tell me you don't trust me."

"I trust you," said Lumati, eyeing the little man very closely, "but I'm not sure I trust your pal, Klein."

"Listen, Lummy," said Sonnley, drawing nearer the artist and looking like an earnest sparrow, "I've worked with Klein for over ten years. They don't come any smarter, but I wouldn't trust him round the corner. Klein's not in this. He's looking after the usual business for me. He's been up in the North and the Midlands, making sure we don't have trouble with those boys. I'll spread your stuff round myself with the takings from my branches, and I'll pay a lot of my bills with them. I'll spread some out with bookies, too. Don't you worry. I'll get rid of most of it in a week. Now, where's the samples?"

Lumati took an envelope from his pocket, and handed it over. Sonnley slit it open, and pulled out the notes inside; there were five. He rustled one in his fingers, put the five down on a table and flipped them like a bank teller. Then he took them to a window, and, standing to one side, held one up to the light. The thread showed through clearly, so did the watermark; it was a remarkable job of printing. He swung round and clapped Lumati on the shoulder.

"That's the best job I've ever seen in my life, Lum! It's an absolute winner."

"It's the best job that's ever been done," said Lumati. His little beard waggled in his excitement. "And I've got fifteen thousand of them. It's a deal, then. You won't tell Klein—"

"Cross my heart."

"You pay me fifty per cent of the face value, on delivery."

"Lum, just to show how much I trust you, I've brought three thousand quid in real English dough along with me —it's in that little case over there. Don't get it mixed up with your own speciality, will you? I wouldn't like to get yours contaminated!" Sonnley went over and picked up a small leather case, opened it, and showed the small wads of one-pound notes, wrapped in fifties with gummed paper bands. "How about that, Lum? You get three thousand quid on account."

Lumati stared down at the money, his eyes glistening, his mouth dry, his lips parted.

When Sonnley left, soon afterwards, he was whistling as merrily as could be, his green Tyrolean hat stuck jauntily on one side of his head. He whistled all the way home, all the way up to Rosie, and all the time he was washing his hands before lunch. He was half-way through a steamed steak-and-kidney pudding of mouth-watering succulence when the telephone bell rang.

"I'll get it, Sonny," Rosie said, and puffed a few straying hairs away from her nose as she leaned on the table, got up, and waddled across to the telephone in a corner; she knew how Sonny Boy disliked being interrupted when he was eating.

"Hello, who's that?" she inquired disinterestedly, and then she said: "Oh, Mrs. Whittaker, hallo, dear, how are you?... Well, I *am* sorry... Well I never... Well, what a funny thing to happen. Has he tried olive oil? It's ever so soothing... Oh, I see... Well, he's busy now, dear—" She glanced across at Sonnley, who was scooping up a forkful of succulent brown meat and gravy-soaked suet crust. He waved his knife at her, and she went on: "He's just come in, dear, wait a minute." She covered the mouthpiece with her podgy hand as she called to Sonnley: "Dicky Whittaker's burnt his hands something cruel. He's had to go to a doctor."

"The damn fool, he's due to start work next week," Sonnley said disgustedly, and grabbed the telephone. "Sonnley speaking. What's all this about...?"

He broke off, listening more intently, and when he spoke again his voice was subdued and the expression in his eyes was very different, and very thoughtful.

"All right, tell him not to worry, I'll stake him," he said curtly, and rang off. He stared at his wife, who sat down placidly although she had just learned that one of the cleverest pickpockets in the business had burned his hands so badly that he would not be able to operate during the Visit.

Someone had smeared vitriol on the handle-bars of his motor-scooter.

When Klein came into his office, next morning, Sonnley sat reading some letters, without looking up. Klein stood by the desk for two minutes, then deliberately sat on a corner. Sonnley took no notice. Klein took out cigarettes, lit one, and dropped the spent match into an ash-tray close to Sonnley's right hand.

"Remember me?" he said.

"I've got to have some bad luck," Sonnley still read.

"You said it," said Klein, flatly. "I've got news for you."

Sonnley looked straight into his eyes for the first time, paused, and then asked:

"What news?"

Sonnley never admitted it to a soul, but Klein's answer took him completely by surprise, and almost broke up his poker face. The answer was one word, spoken with that guttural accent, taking on a kind of menace which Sonnley had not known for a long time.

"Cops," said Klein.

Sonnley needed a moment's respite, and he said:

"What's that?"

"Cops."

"What the hell do you mean, cops?"

"I mean busies, dicks, bloody flatfoots," said Klein. "They're watching my van. They followed me this morning. There's a couple outside now—one of them was at the station when I got back last night, one was outside here when I arrived. Think he was waiting to pass the time of day with me? What have you been doing?"

"I don't believe—" Sonnley began.

"You take a look," invited Klein.

Sonnley stood up, slowly, and went to the window. He had lost his perkiness and heartiness as he stood at one side of the window, to avoid being seen. On the other side of the street, standing by a telephone kiosk and reading a newspaper, was a tall, heavily-built man, and Sonnley knew that Klein was right. There was another, taller, thinner man, strolling along the street.

"What have you been up to, to bring them as close as this?" demanded Klein.

"It's just routine," Sonnley said uneasily. "That's all it can be."

"Okay, then, it's just routine," said Klein. "But if I start collecting the stuff from the boys and girls and get copped, I'll be back on the Moor, and that's a routine I don't like. I've got some more news for you."

"Now, listen, Benny—"

"I want out," said Klein. "I want five thousand quid as a golden handshake, and then I'll just fade out of your life. I'm not taking any more chances, and it's time I got my bonus."

Sonnley returned to his desk, sat down, and looked into the other man's bright grey eyes. There was nothing there that he liked, nothing remotely reassuring. He had known that one day a break would come, but he hadn't expected blackmail, and he hadn't expected it to come so suddenly. He took out a check green and white handkerchief, and dabbed at his forehead. Klein didn't shift his gaze. He had one hand clenched on the desk, another with the palm upwards, the fingers crooked and beckoning.

"Give," he said.

Sonnley still didn't speak. Klein leaned across the desk so that Sonnley could feel the warmth of his breath, and repeated:

"Give."

Sonnley said thinly: "Not a penny."

"Say that again, and I'll break your neck."

"Then you'll go inside for the rest of your life."

Klein's eyes narrowed, as if he hadn't anticipated such tough resistance.

"Sonny Boy, don't get me wrong," he said. "I want out

146

and I want five thousand quid, and that's how it's going to be."

"Benny," said Sonnley, in a voice which shook a little, "you aren't going to get another penny from me unless you see the next ten days through. You can please yourself."

Klein was towering over him, lips drawn back. There was silence and stillness in the room for what seemed a very long time, and with every second it looked as if Klein would explode into action. Before he did, while the breath was hissing through his mouth, Sonnley said in a soft voice:

"Who smeared vitriol on Dicky Whittaker's motor-scooter?"

For a moment Klein's expression did not change; he still looked as if he would burst into violent action. Then he blinked. He closed his lips, moistened them, and said:

"What's that?" and drew back a pace, as if his rage had suddenly died away. "*What's* that?"

"You heard."

"Come again."

"Who smeared vitriol on the handle-bars of Dicky Whittaker's motor-scooter?"

"Someone did *that*?" Klein sighed.

"You've been back in London since last night, and no one told you?"

Klein said, still sighingly: "You're telling me, aren't you?" He moistened his lips again. "Because the cops were watching, I kept away from all the boys. I didn't hear anything. Sonny Boy, is this right?"

"It's right."

"Then Dicky can't work."

"He can't work."

Klein said: "Who did it, that's what I want to know? Who did it?"

"That's what I want to know too," said Sonnley. "If you want out and five thousand quid, you find out who did it."

"Who would hate Dicky as much as that?"

"Just find out, and let me know quick," said Sonnley, "because when I find out who did it, I'll break him. Understand?" He stared levelly, coldly, into Klein's eyes. "Whoever it was, I'll break him for good. Just remember that."

"I'll find him," Klein said. "I'll find the swine."

Sonnley watched as he turned away and went out, and saw no change in his expression. Sonnley jumped up from the desk, stepped swiftly to the door, pulled it open, and saw Klein half-way across the room beyond, still looking astounded; if he knew more than he pretended, he was covering it well. Did he know? Or was he as shocked as he made out?

Sonnley went back to his desk, sat down, then jumped up again and took three jerky steps to the window. The watcher by the kiosk hadn't moved, but the taller, thinner man was now farther along the street. Klein appeared on the pavement. The thin man turned and followed him. Sonnley watched them both go round the corner. The man by the telephone kiosk stayed put, which meant that Klein had been right, and that he, Sonnley, was being watched.

Sonnley's lips pursed, and he began to whistle, but it was a thin, grating sound, with no high spirits, no attempt to catch a tune. Now he had two problems, two big problems, and he had to decide which needed priority.

The question of priorities was Gideon's chief preoccupation, too, and it became more acute as the days passed. A week before the Visit, it seemed as if there was an impossible amount to do; masses of paperwork passed over his desk, and for days he hardly moved out of the office. That worsened his feelings of frustration and strengthened the urge to get out and about; but he could not, wisely. He was a little sore because he had advised Cox to go round to all the Divisions and check the arrangements and the men to be released for Central London work, and instead of jumping at it, Cox had looked down his nose as if it were a chore. But that side of the arrangements appeared to be working smoothly, and he did not allow it to worry him; he was getting used to Cox.

On the Monday before the Visit he spent less time than usual looking through reports and briefing his men, but a note from Abbott caught his eye. *"Beryl Belman will be here today—would you like to see her?"* Gideon looked across at Bell, and said:

"Tell Abby I'll go down and have a word with the Belman girl, will you?"

"Right."

"Anything more on Carraway?"

"Absolutely blank, Abby says—it's like coming up against a brick wall."

One of Gideon's telephones rang, and he lifted it while glancing at another report. It was Christy of N.E. Division.

"Yes, Hugh?"

"Funny thing happened you ought to know about," said Christy, without preamble. "Remember Dicky Whittaker?" On the instant Gideon pictured a tall, very thin, sorrowful-looking man, who had often been inside for picking pockets and snatching handbags; he was probably the cleverest man in London at either job.

"I remember him."

"He's burned the skin off his hands. Someone smeared his scooter handles wih vitriol, and put him out of business."

Gideon gave a snort, smothering a laugh.

"Well, who's complaining?"

"I'm just telling you," Christy said. "While I'm on, George—half a mo'." Christy wasn't a man to waste time, so Gideon scanned another report and started on a third before Christy came back. "One of my chaps got punched on the nose by a drunk, he's just come in . . . What was I going to say?"

"You tell me."

"Oh, yes—I had Ray Cox here last night. Kept me here until half past ten, the so-and-so."

"Did he?" Gideon asked, mildly.

"Seems to be right on the ball," said Christy. "He knows exactly what he wants and how to get it, if you ask me. Thought you'd like to know you're in good hands! 'Bye."

Christy rang off, and Gideon put his receiver down slowly, rubbed his nose, shrugged, and went on with his reports. But his spirits rose a little; that was the first cheering report he'd had about Cox.

His telephone bell rang again, and Abbott said:

"Beryl B's downstairs in the waiting-room, George. I don't think she can help us over Carraway, though—but she can put Little away."

Gideon was surprised by the girl's attractiveness, her feathery hair, and the likeness to her dead sister. She looked pale, her eyes were very bright, and she spoke in a subdued voice while looking him straight in the eyes. He felt quite sure that she was telling the truth when she said that she had wanted to see Carraway, but had never met him.

Gideon talked for ten minutes or so, and then stood up.

"I'm sure Mr. Abbott's told you how sorry we are about what happened, Miss Belman. If we can do anything to help you, or your parents, let Mr. Abbott know."

"He's been ever so kind, sir," said Beryl earnestly. "My father says he'll always respect the police much more than he used to, after this. Mr. Abbott's been ever so good to me, too, and I would like to thank him personally."

Abbott was almost preening himself, Gideon saw. He would make the grade now, so one uncertainty was past, and the morning's upward trend continued.

Gideon went out, feeling as if the weight was lifting. He was much more cheerful when he opened the door of his office, and was surprised to see Violet Timson at his desk. She moved away from it quickly, almost guiltily?

"I was looking for a report on the Little case, sir, for the Assistant Commissioner," she said. "Mr. Bell's out, too."

Her cheeks were flushed, and she sounded as if she expected a sharp rebuke. If he gave one, it would undo all the work done towards a better understanding, so he simply said:

"You'll find it on his desk."

"Oh, how silly of me. Thank you," she said hurriedly, and went across to the other desk and picked up the file. "Mr. Rogerson wants to talk to the Solicitor's Office about another remand." She went out briskly.

Gideon put his hand in his pocket, then smoothed the bowl of his pipe, and stared at the papers. He saw one thin file which wasn't quite squared with the others, pulled it out, and read: *Australian Party*. She had been checking to find out if there was any further news of Wall. Well, there wasn't. He smiled thoughtfully to himself, and put the report aside, wondering how serious the *affaire* was going to be.

He had been alone for ten minutes when there were brisk footsteps outside, and before the sharp, peremptory knock came at the door, he knew this was Cox.

He steeled himself.

"Come in."

Cox came in, briskly, glanced at Bell's empty desk, advanced to Gideon's, and said:

"Good morning, Commander. I think we've got everything we need, now. Plenty of reserves, the Divisions all organized for the first three days of next week, everything laid on." He was hearty, and brisker than usual, as if making a big effort to create a mood of *camaraderie*. "There are two things I'd like your advice on."

This was sensational.

"Pull up a chair—" Gideon began.

"I won't, if you don't mind. I'm going over to the City in five minutes, just called in on my way." Cox put papers on Gideon's desk. "Do you think it would be a good idea if we—you and I, I mean, personally—did a kind of tour of inspection together later in the week, or next week-end? Keep everyone on their toes, and make sure that nothing slips up."

Gideon said: "Anything that would take me out of this

blurry office is right with me. We'll fix two separate half-days, shall we?"

"Whenever you say," said Cox. He was very newly shaven, his eyes were bright, his long thin neck and jutting ears made him look just a little comical. "The other thing is really something to be tackled at Divisional level, but in order to be at full strength next week a lot of leave is being taken this week. The Divisions are pretty short of men." This was elementary. "There's a missing neighbour case down in Streatham." Streatham was one of London's older, more sedate suburbs, in a quiet Division. "A woman's been missing for several days, and a neighbour's been worrying the sub-divisional station, because there's a heap of fresh soil in the garden. As a matter of fact, I would have recommended that the Division goes and digs that soil over, but if I'd asked Miller for anything else I think he would have snapped my head off."

"I know what you mean," said Gideon. At least one Divisional Superintendent disagreed with Hugh Christy on Cox's merits. "Uniform reported it, and Divisional C.I.D. is sitting on it. That right?"

"Yes."

"Give me the name and address," said Gideon. "I'll pick it up from a Divisional report—there's bound to be one—and ask Jeff Miller to have that plot dug over. He can get a warrant on the grounds that we're looking for stolen goods. Job like that shouldn't take long. If the earth's fresh and there's been no effort to cover it over, I wouldn't expect to find much there. What's the name?"

Cox answered almost blithely :

"The woman's a Grace Smith, Mrs. Grace Smith. Miller says that the husband's a sour piece of work, and thinks that this is just a neighbour's spitefulness. Just as well to be sure, though."

Cox spoke like a schoolboy who was very conscious of good behaviour.

"You couldn't be more right," Gideon said.

He called Miller, of the Division, and Miller—preoccupied with some other problem—promised to get the warrant at once. Gideon expected to have to remind him, but within three hours the report came in. *Soil at 41, Common Road dug over as requested. Result, negative.*

"All right as far as it goes," Gideon said to Bell. "But where did the soil come from? Put in a call, and ask Miller, will you?" He sorted through some papers, as he went on : "Did our Vi bring that Little file back?"

"She brought it in full of apologies," answered Bell. "If it wasn't for that Aussie I'd think she had quite a crush on you."

Undoubtedly Donnelly and Webron were anxious, but they had the comfort of knowing that every possible action was being taken in London to trace O'Hara, and by now they had some idea how thorough the check would be, from top men in the Divisions down to the youngest flatfoots on the beat. It would not have surprised them to know, for instance, that Police Constable Kemp was very thoughtful about the wanted American.

Kemp had come to know which of the hotel managers and manageresses of the smaller establishments were helpful. From time to time he had to go and check the registers of guests, and this was the excuse he made when he called at the Lambett Guest House on the following morning. He saw the name Hann in the book which Mrs. Lambett showed him. She was a pleasant, if somewhat reserved woman, who charged more than most and catered for a better type of guest.

"Now this Mr. Hann, he's an American, I see," Kemp remarked. "Here for the Summit, is he?"

"I understand that he is planning a long holiday in Europe, and England is his first stop," answered Mrs. Lambett.

"Nice chap?" asked Kemp.

"He is a very satisfactory guest."

"I know one thing, these Americans can afford a lot more on cameras than I ever could," said Kemp. "How many's he got? Two or three?" He made a joke of it.

"As far as I know, he has only one, a ciné camera," replied Mrs. Lambett.

Without pressing too hard, Kemp could not learn more from her, but he did find out that Hann was coming in for a midday meal. So he made it his business to watch the street, and saw Hann turn from the corner of the High Street, without knowing for sure who he was; but he did see a likeness, if a vague one, to the photograph. He also saw the camera, and thought it looked big enough for a sixteen millimetre.

At the station, Kemp checked on the details of O'Hara's description; height and weight were about right, but this man's hair was jet black, not pale brown turning grey. The possibility that it was dyed made him suspicious. He reported to the C.I.D. branch at the Division, but the sergeant who took the report said disparagingly:

"That's five we've had from here alone. The Yard must be flooded out."

"That's up to them," said Kemp. "I've done my bit."

17

KILLER-CAMERA

GIDEON stood in the doorway of the *Information Room,* watching, listening to men's quiet voices, the tap-tap-tap of the teleprint machines, the subdued buzzing of bells. Nowhere was the ceaseless activity of the Yard more evident than here. At the long desks with the conveyor belt running between them, carrying urgent messages so unhurriedly, uniformed men sat with casual-seeming intentness.

No one seemed to hurry, but the pace was always steady, and much faster than it seemed.

A man was saying :

"Two youths, age about nineteen, robbed a grocery shop in Whitechapel at 2.31 p.m. and got away with seventeen pounds one shilling. No description available."

Another was taking a different message :

"Two private cars were in collision at the north end of Lambeth Bridge at 2.32 p.m., both cars badly damaged, one driver dead, the other injured. Traffic has been reduced to single line . . ."

A third message came over the teleprinter as Gideon watched the tape ticking through.

"Attempted bank robbery at Lloyds Bank, Richmond, Surrey, at 2.30 p.m., two men and a girl involved. A bank clerk raised the alarm. The girl and one man have been held, the other man escaped with a bag containing about two thousand three hundred pounds in used treasury notes . . ."

The messages were distributed to the departments concerned without comment. Within a few minutes Bell would be checking with Division about the bank raid ; it looked as if that had failed, so luck was holding.

Another message came through on the machine :

"Message from C.D. Division." That was from Kensington and Cromwell Road area. "Police Constable R. E. Kemp reports an American who might fit the description of the man O'Hara. He says that this suspect's hair is jet black and looks as if it might have been recently dyed. The man is staying at the Lambett Guest House under the name of Hann."

The Chief Inspector in charge of *Information* came up and said :

"Another O'Hara false alarm."

"One of them's going to be the McCoy sooner or later," replied Gideon. "That gone up to Donnelly and Webron?"

"It's on its way."

"Thanks," said Gideon. "I can see I'm not needed down here."

In fact, all the Yard was fairly quiet because of the lull in major crime, and the day-to-day commonplaces could almost look after themselves. It was just the right afternoon for a jaunt, and it would do no harm to go out with Donnelly and Webron. They would then be able to report back to Washington that the Commander in person was concentrating on O'Hara. Smiling at his own humbug, Gideon went upstairs to the Americans' office, and found it empty. A sergeant, passing by, said :

"The two Yanks have just gone out, sir."

"Oh," said Gideon. He didn't like "Yanks" but one could overdo punctiliousness. He thought ruefully that the pair hadn't lost a moment ; that was probably a measure of their anxiety. He lifted a telephone, called Bell, and said :

"Joe, I'm going out for a stretch—over to take a look at that latest O'Hara."

"Enjoy yourself," said Bell.

Gideon went downstairs, to find a chauffeur at the foot of the steps ; Bell had uncanny ability in arranging that. Gideon told the driver where to go, and sat beside him, watching the traffic, studying the quick reactions, knowing that at one time this man had been a star driver of the Flying Squad ; he was now nearing sixty.

"In a hurry, sir ?" he asked.

"We needn't break our necks," Gideon said.

He was glad to be out, no matter what the excuse, and quite expected to find two disappointed Americans when he reached the Division.

Little more than half an hour after P.C. Kemp had made his report, Donnelly and Webron reached the corner of the street where the Lambett Hotel was, Webron at the wheel of a grey Austin Cambridge. They waited for twelve minutes, before a larger car turned into the street, and as it passed, Webron exclaimed in surprise :

"There's the great Gideon."

"I don't believe it," Donnelly scoffed.

"You'll believe it," Webron said. "Does he know anything more?" He opened the door of the car and got out as Gideon's car stopped.

Gideon glanced up at the newly painted private building, with *Lambett Hotel* painted shiny black on big white columns, then glanced along and saw Webron. He waved, and strolled towards him, looking huge against the stocky American, whose dark hair was ruffled by a strong wind, and who looked up with a half grin.

"Special information ?" he inquired.

"No. I just thought that dyed hair worth looking at," explained Gideon. "Do you know if Hann's in ?"

"He's in," said Webron. "Your Divisional man has been watching, and he told us ; he's put two men at each corner."

"We don't want anything to happen to our guests," Gideon said drily. He watched his car moving along, and strolled after it, content to feel the pavement solid beneath his feet. It carried him back twenty-nine years, to that time when he had first pounded a beat, and there was a positive nostalgia about it.

He heard a soft toot on a car horn, and glanced round.

A man was turning away from the Lambett Hotel. He

was of medium height, with jet black hair, and had a camera slung over his shoulder. Hebron was only a few yards in front of him. Donnelly was getting out of the car into the road, and a small van, coming along fast, honked its horn wildly. Donnelly dodged back. Gideon swung round and began to stride towards the stranger, and as he did so, he saw Webron's expression change, and saw horror on Donnelly's face as he rounded the car. Although the suspect had his back turned to him, Gideon saw the swift movement of the camera strap and the position of his arms; the man was levelling the camera at Webron, so Webron might be face to face with death.

Gideon opened his mouth and yelled: "*Police!*" He saw the suspect start; he saw Donnelly leap forward, trip on the kerb, and fall headlong. The man with the camera jumped away from him, and Webron dived in turn. In the moment of furious confusion, Gideon was still twenty yards away. He saw the suspect rush towards the porch of the hotel; somehow, Webron flung himself sideways, to stop him. Then the man with the camera jumped towards the steps which led down to the hotel's sub-basement, and managed to slam the waist-high iron gate behind him. He was on one side of the gate, and Donnelly was helpless on the other. Webron was going forward with cold-blooded determination.

The "camera" was trained on them both.

"Get away," Hann said, gaspingly. "Get away from me. Let me go or I'll kill you."

"Stop the talk," Webron said. The edge on his voice told Gideon how tense he was; and how afraid. He took a step nearer. "You've had your day, O'Hara. Just drop that—"

"*Get away from me or I'll shoot you both.*"

"Mr. O'Hara," Gideon called in a level voice. He was only a few yards away, approaching with long, deceptively leisurely strides. Donnelly, picking himself up, glanced at him as if in astonishment, and Webron moved forward again. "It's one thing to assassinate your President, if you believe he is betraying your country," Gideon went on conversationally, "but it's another to commit cold-blooded murder. These men are just doing their job. You might injure them, or even kill them, but you can't get away. The hotel is surrounded, and I can have armed men here in a few minutes." He put a hand to his pocket, calmly, took out his wallet, and extracted a card. "I am Commander Gideon of the Criminal Investigation Department." He held the card forward and saw O'Hara staring at him, lips already beginning to work, strength and purpose failing.

The camera dropped before Gideon touched the man.

"Commander, I just want to tell you that was the coolest nerve I've ever seen in a man," declared Donnelly.

"Amen to that," Webron said.

Gideon sat back in his chair behind his desk, looked from one man to the other, and said :

"That was the biggest slice of luck I've had in years. I couldn't let it slip through my fingers. O'Hara isn't a killer as such. I didn't see how the appeal could fail." He meant exactly what he said. It seemed to him that the day had changed the whole outlook of the Visit; everything had started to go right, and he was positively light-hearted.

Later, when he talked to Kate about the newspaper account of this, he was to say honestly that it had not occurred to him that there was really any danger ; and she was to believe him. Now he went on : "It's our biggest headache over, anyhow." He thought : *I'm a blurry fool. I ought to have told them they had all the guts in the world, too.* But that would be an anti-climax now. "O'Hara's downstairs, praying. We'll charge him with being in possession of a fire-arm without a licence, and that will keep him on remand in custody for eight days. By then we should have an extradition warrant ready. That what you two want ?"

"Commander, that's exactly what we want," Webron replied. "Is there anything we can do for you ?"

"Yes," said Gideon. "Go out to Kensington, and have a word with Constable Kemp."

"We'll be glad to," said Webron. "Is there any rule against taking him out to dinner?"

"Make it a good dinner," Gideon urged.

On that same evening, Matthew Smith turned into the gateway of his house, went round the side as he usually did, hesitated at the back door, and then went towards the workshop. He did not even glance towards the heap of soil which he had dug up from beneath the workshop, and did not yet know that it had been examined; his neighbours were not likely to tell him. He did not notice that the woman next door was watching him through a window.

He unlocked the workshop door, stepped inside, glanced at the spot where his dead wife lay, and quickly looked away. Thought of her vanished from his mind as he stared at the hiding-place where he kept the bomb. His heart began to pound, and blood throbbed through his ears. It was so very near; the great moment was almost in his grasp. He could not wait to take that bomb and hurl it at the hated creature in the gilded coach. He could not wait to hear the roar of the explosion, to see the horses rear up, to see a devil being blown to pieces. He did not give a thought to the people who would be in the stand behind him.

On the Saturday, the day London would be flooded with visitors, and the first day intended for a series of widespread raids by Sonnley's men. Sonnley had not whistled much in the past few days. He was worried, although there were some reasons for thinking that the worst of his worries might be over. The police were taking comparatively little notice of him, and he knew that they were stretched very thin. Probably the watching earlier in the week had been in an effort to scare him and Klein.

He did not know what to make of Klein.

After the news of the "accident" to Whittaker, Klein

seemed to have become obsessed with the idea of finding out who had smeared those handle-bars, but he had failed. No other burnt fingers had been reported, and as far as Sonnley's scouts in the big provincial cities knew, there was no movement towards London. Klein seemed to have paid them to stay out of the big smoke, as instructed, and that was just as Sonnley wanted it.

But how far could he trust Klein?

He told himself that Klein was reliable at least until he had been paid off, but would have to be watched very carefully afterwards. Meanwhile, Sonnley double-checked his own arrangements for the Visit.

He meant to have an alibi which no one could possibly break. He had to make sure that the money was collected and paid into the bank quickly, and that the stolen goods were moved quickly, too. He also wanted to distribute Lumati's money—he had collected it days ago, and it was stored in the cellar of one of his shops—but for a reason which he could not explain to himself, he held that back. He had collected it, and it was safely stached away. There was no hurry with the money, and the police might be on the look-out for forged notes.

At the back of Sonnley's mind, there was one way in which he could use the slush, but his immediate concern was to see that his own plans worked smoothly.

On the Saturday morning, he gave Rosie a peck of a kiss, and went outside. It was bright and sunny, and by the time he reached the garage at the back of the flats he was whistling cheerfully; good weather was just what his "artists" wanted. He slid into the driving-seat, switched on the ignition, and took the wheel. Immediately he felt something sticky and wet, that puzzled him for a moment. Then, only seconds before the acid began to burn, he realized what it was.

He snatched his hands away, and sat absolutely still, eyes glaring, hands crooked, the burning pain worse with every passing second. Soon he made choking noises in his throat, as if he were fighting for breath.

That day, the day which should have been Sonny Boy Sonnley's greatest harvest, his "artists" left home for the West End of London, each of them very careful with the handle-bars of bicycles, scooters and motor-cycles; none of them used cars, because of the need for quick getaways. All of them went among the crowds for the first of their jobs. The weather was so lovely that it made the people happy and careless, and pockets and handbags were easy game. In all, fourteen of the men made good first pickings, and hurried back to their machines.

Exactly the same thing happened in each case, in dozens of different places.

Each man gripped the handle-bars, and started off; after a few seconds, each man pulled into the kerb, snatched his hands from the bars and looked down. Each saw hands and fingers which were already red and blistering, and which were beginning to cause agony.

Man after man jumped off his machine, bystanders staring at them as they waved their hands about wildly.

The police were soon alerted.

Superintendent Lemaitre pulled up in his blue Humber outside Gideon's front door, early that afternoon, and Gideon saw him from the bedroom, where he was mending a spring blind. Kate was out shopping. Gideon was on call, and judging from Lemaitre's expression, this was an urgent one. He smiled to himself as Lemaitre disappeared along the path, and carried a mind-picture of the tall, thin, rather gawkish man, with spotted red-and-white bow-tie, grey overcheck suit which somehow contrived to be loud, and narrow-brimmed trilby set at a jaunty angle on the side of his head.

The bell rang twice before Gideon could get to the door.

"In a hurry, Lem?" he asked mildly.

"In a blurry hurry," Lemaitre cracked, and there was excitement but not anxiety in his eyes. "Gottabitta news for you." He came in, almost as familiar with the house as Gideon, and went on boisterously: "Remember old

Dicky Whittaker? Poor old Dicky with the blistered fingers?"

"Well?"

"We've had nine cases of blistered fingers reported this afternoon," Lemaitre announced, joyfully. "Every one of them a Klein and Sonny Boy man! How about that, George?" Without giving Gideon a chance to respond, Lemaitre careered on, taking a slip of paper from his pocket. "Every one of the baskets was caught with his pockets stuffed with loot, too. Every one's a dead cert for three years inside, after hospital treatment. Some of their hands—you should see! Raw isn't the word. But the thing is, George, I know what's on."

Gideon said cautiously : "Do you?"

"That's right, that's right, tell me I'm jumping to con-clusions again. This time I'm bang on the ball." Lemaitre waved the slip of paper in front of Gideon's nose. "Now listen to me, George. Here is a list of the boys who've been burnt. They can't work, understand? One might have been an accident, but nine makes a campaign, and there may be more to come. So as soon as I heard there were several of them, I checked round with the provincial cities. You want to know something?"

"Try me."

"Jock Gorra's boys left Glasgow last night and this morning. Some by train, some by road. And remember, Klein was up there, with Gorra, and they behaved like dear old pals. You can take it from me, the Glasgow Blacks are coming to take over from Sonnley, and all we've got to do is pick 'em up as they arrive, and have 'em sent back to Glasgow. Now wait a minute, wait a minute!" pleaded Lemaitre, as Gideon tried to get a word in. "I've telephoned Glasgow. They've put out an official request for all of Gorra's gang to be sent back for questioning. It's only a matter of finding them. They won't be likely to come by road, not all the way, it's a hell of a drive. I think those who started out by road will catch a train further south, maybe in Carlisle, and we ought to be able to pick them up at Euston."

"Got the stations watched yet?" demanded Gideon.

"Attaboy," said Lemaitre, and his grin seemed to split his face in two. "I've done better—action, that's me. We got seven of the so-and-so's off the *Flying Scot*, and nine more at the Victoria Coach Station. Don't they hate London!"

Gideon joined in his laugh, and felt a deep satisfaction.

His hands bandaged and free from pain, Sonnley was sitting at the window of his apartment, staring down into the street. Now and again he muttered harshly :

"I'll get the swine. I'll get him."

Most people in London were happy, however, and among these was a certain Arthur Ritter, from Worcester, who was driving a car hired from Carraway without caring what it cost. At that time, he was alone.

So was Doris Green.

18

TICKETS FOR THE STAND

LITTLE Doris Green, pretty in her new flowered hat, was not happy; in fact she was scared.

She had been to London twice, each time with her mother, who was now dead; her father had been dead for many years. She stood forlorn and lonely on that Saturday evening. The soft light gentled the rather hard green of her tweed suit, a neat and fashionable little outfit. She looked nice. Somehow the cut of the jacket and the high neck of the yellowish blouse beneath it emphasized the roundness of her bosom and the smallness of her waist. She wore flesh-coloured stockings on legs which were rather too full at the calf, thus accentuating her small ankles and brown-clad feet.

Along the row of tall, grey, porticoed houses in Cromwell Road were the signs one after another: *No Vacancy. Full. Sorry, Full Up.* Two youths walked past her, turned, and walked past again. A coloured man stood on the other side of the wide road, looking at her. Massive red buses and little dark cars would cut him off from sight momentarily, and back he would come again. A sports car slowed down, and a man with a black wavy moustache called:

"Like a ride, baby?"

One of the youths, approaching for the third time, called: "How about a bit o' rock-on'-roll, doll?"

Doris was more than ever scared, and walked quickly along towards a traffic junction and another busy road. At the corner, a dozen people surged off the pavement and she was nearly bowled over. She recovered, went with the crowd, and was knocked from the far side. When she felt a tug at her left arm, she thought nothing of it until she reached the far pavement. Then she discovered that her handbag was gone.

She was so shocked that she stood absolutely rigid. People pushed past her, a man said "Sorry", another growled: "Want all the pavement?" She moved towards the side of a house, staring blankly at her left wrist, where the bag had been hanging.

In a strangled voice, she said: "No, oh, no."

Then tears filled her eyes; she had to fight against crying out. She had no idea who had stolen the bag, no idea what to do; she was beyond thought.

For in that bag was thirty pounds; every penny she had.

Arthur Ritter had been a widower for seven years. He was rather shorter than average, stocky, with iron grey hair, a young face, and clear brown eyes. He dressed well and walked well. He owned a small pottery near Worcester, was comfortably off, had no particular vices and few of what he would recognize as virtues. Now and again, because he was lonely, he visited a woman in a town near his home; he always came away feeling a little ashamed.

That Saturday evening, he had driven from his hotel near Piccadilly to see an old friend in a guest house in the Cromwell Road. His car was parked a hundred yards away, and walking towards it after visiting his friend, he noticed the girl in the green suit and the little flowery hat on a mop of golden-coloured hair. He noticed the two youths and the man in the car, too, and felt annoyed with them and sorry for the girl. She looked so forlorn. He saw when she crossed the road, noticed the youth who bumped into her, and saw him quicken his pace and then turn a corner. A moment later, the girl stumbled, and two more men bumped into her. She went to the side of a big house with round, cream-coloured pillars and a high porch, and looked as if she could stand no more.

Everyone else ignored her.

Ritter went towards her, feeling awkward and shy, and yet genuinely sorry for her. He stood a yard or two away, close enough to see the tears glistening on her eyelashes.

He could keep quiet no longer.

"Excuse me," he said, with a frog in his throat. "Excuse me, but—can I help you?"

She stared at him without speaking, her lovely violet eyes still glistening.

"I don't want to butt in, but—I'll be glad to help if I can."

Hesitantly, tremulously, she told him what had happened.

It was a strange, touching little encounter, a father-and-daughter-like meeting. She mustn't worry, she mustn't cry. He would see the police for her. She would almost certainly get her money back. He would find out where the police station was. Where was she staying?

"*Nowhere!*" he exclaimed. "You mean your home isn't in London?"

"No."

"And you've nowhere to stay?"

Pathetically, she said: "And I haven't got any money, either."

The police at a nearby sub-station were affable but not really hopeful; and of course they asked for Doris's address. Almost without thinking, Ritter said:

"The Welchester Hotel."

"What room number, please?"

"Seven-o-seven." He gave his own, for there was no other to give.

"Look here, my dear," he said, when they were outside. "I'll lend you some money. I'll be happy to."

"It's ever so kind of you, but—"

"Look here, young lady," said Ritter, suddenly masterful, "you can't wander around London without any money and without anywhere to sleep. We'll go and find you a hotel for the night, anyhow. I'll drive, and you look out for a place on your side."

No Vacancy. Full. Full Up. No Rooms. Fully Booked, the signs read, and it was dark by the time they had given up.

167

"You *must* have somewhere to sleep," Ritter said, desperately. "Perhaps my hotel has a room."

He took her there. As they approached the Reception Desk through the crowded foyer, three applicants for rooms were turned away.

"You *can't* stay out all night," he said, in a funny kind of voice, for by then he was beginning to realize what might come of this. "I can't allow it. You—you must have my room."

"Oh, I can't possibly !"

Instinct or premonition told him that she could and she would, and in his heart he knew exactly what was going to happen. His conscience worried him a little because she was so young, but she wasn't a *child*.

"I'll tell you what," he said. "There's a settee up there."

She was shaken and scared and lonely, and he was old enough to be her father. She was not at all frightened of him.

His bedroom was more luxurious than any room she had ever been in. There was a bathroom, too, and the settee was plenty long enough for her. He wanted her to take the bed, but she refused, almost gaily. He sent for some sandwiches, and she hid in the bathroom when the waiter brought them. When she came out, they laughed conspiratorially.

Arthur locked and bolted the passage door. *Arthur* went into the bathroom while Doris slipped off her clothes and put on a pair of his pyjamas. *Arthur* came out, breathing a little fast and roughly. He went over to her, and bent over her, and leaned down and kissed her, softly—gently —passionately.

It was the first time that Doris had known a man. Ritter knew that, as he took her so gently yet so daringly, so guiltily, and yet with such ecstasy.

"Of course I'm not ashamed," Doris said, next morning. "Arthur, you mustn't be, either. I-I-I *loved* being with you."

They did not leave the room until nearly twelve o'clock, and they walked out together, as in a dream. Near the hotel an office was open, selling stand tickets for the Procession, the lowest price left being twelve guineas each. Ritter bought two; he would have bought them at double or treble the price.

Alec Sonnley went out by himself, to collect the tickets for the Procession stand. When he had them, he went to a telephone booth and, with great difficulty, inserted the coppers and dialled the number where he expected to find Klein. It rang on and on for a long time, while he scowled straight ahead at people passing in the street. Nothing would go right.

Then the ringing stopped, and Klein answered:

"Benny Klein speaking."

"Benny," Sonnley said, in a low-pitched voice; he managed to make himself sound anxious.

"Who's that?" demanded Klein, and then caught his breath. "Is that you, Sonny Boy?"

"Listen, Benny," said Sonnley, with soft urgency, "I know who fixed that acid now. It was that flicker from Glasgow, Jock Gorra. I can't do anything to Gorra yet, but the day will come. Listen, Benny—"he broke off.

"I'm listening," Klein said, as if he could not really believe that Sonnley was affable.

"I'm throwing my hand in," Sonnley declared. "I can't take any more of it, Benny. I'm past it. So I'm throwing my hand in, and I want to make sure the cops don't get anything on me over the grapevine. I want you to keep your mouth shut about me, Benny."

Klein said, swiftly: "What's it worth, Sonny Boy?"

That was the moment when Sonnley felt sure that Klein had taken the bait, and after a long pause he smiled for the first time since his fingers had been burned. Then he said anxiously:

"We agreed on five thou', didn't we?"

"*How* much, Sonny Boy?"

"Five thou'—"

169

"It's a deal for ten thousand," Klein said. "Ten thousand will make a lot of difference to me, but a rich man like you won't notice it." There was a sneer in his voice.

Sonnley muttered: "I'm not so rich, but—well, I don't want trouble, Benny. I'll make it ten. But my hands are all burned up, you'll have to collect it. You'll find it in the cellar at the Norvil Street shop. It's packed in television set cartons—I thought I'd need plenty of change. You've got some keys, haven't you?"

"I've got some keys," Benny said. "Okay, Sonny Boy, you can sleep easy."

When he stepped out of the telephone booth, Sonnley stood for a moment, wiping his forehead with the back of one bandaged hand. Then he turned towards his home. His lips puckered as he began to whistle.

On the Sunday morning, Mildred Cox got up first, glad that Ray was asleep. She had never known him so tired, never known work take so much out of him; in a way, he had been worse at home since she had persuaded him to try to get on with Gideon. She knew the truth, of course; he could never bear to play second fiddle, yet something about Gideon made him feel inferior.

He slept until ten o'clock; when he woke he was irritable and sharp-voiced, so that young Tom was subdued.

"I'm going to check progress along the route," he told Mildred. "I can't be sure when I'll be home."

He drove to Parliament Square, where the flags were up, and the flowers at the window-boxes of the government buildings were at their loveliest. Crowds were already thronging the streets. Cars were parked beyond the various barricades. Traffic was already too thick to allow it in Whitehall, Parliament Square, St. James's Park or the Mall. Cox recognized a lot of C.I.D. men mixing with the crowds, and wasn't surprised to see Parsons.

"About what you'd expect today," Parsons remarked when they met. "Half the pickpockets and bag snatchers in London. But the big boys aren't out—you heard what happened?"

"Eh? Oh, the acid."

"That's it," said Parsons, drily. "And the Glasgow boys have been sent off, with fleas in their ears. You all right?"

"Can't see anything I've missed," Cox said, rather tartly.

"Tell you one thing I forgot," said Parsons. "Gee-Gee asked me if your wife would like a stand ticket for Wednesday. He'll be glad to fix it."

After a fight between a cool rejection and Mildred's interest, Cox said : "She'd like one very much."

There was much activity on that Sunday in other parts of London, and in Paris, Bonn and New York.

The airport security measures were checked for the last time, and Gideon drove to London Airport to see a rehearsal. Airport police and officials were with him at the control tower.

He watched ground crews, airport maintenance men, rescue service squads, both fire and medical, going through their drill with satisfying precision and speed. From lift-boy to door attendant, news-stand assistant and restaurant worker, everyone had been screened. All scheduled aircraft were re-routed or re-timed, to keep the air, runways and services clear for the three Presidents and their retinues. Two helicopters were detailed to keep continual surveillance. Watch-tower crews were doubled. The pilots of the four aircraft concerned were briefed by radio-telephone down to the most minute detail. Security men and women, as well as police, were stationed at every possible danger-point. The roof-top Observation Point was closely checked, too, and officials stationed there. The day-by-day and hour-by-hour routine of the airport was set aside. Few officials minded, but passengers complained bitterly in all tongues from English to Finnish, from Urdu to Japanese.

Satisfied as far as he could be, Gideon joined Cox, as arranged. He sensed the man's tautness; but at least he was civil and even overdid his thanks for the stand ticket.

They checked as the greater London Police Forces went

into action along the route from the airport to the embassies and hotels, drove the whole route, where men were stationed every hundred yards or so. They drove over the roads to be closed, too, so as to make sure the main route could not be affected on the big day itself.

"Don't think we've missed much," Gideon said, when they had finished. "How about a drink, Ray?"

After a startled pause, Cox said: "I could do with a pint. Thanks."

In and near the embassies, Security keyed itself to the biggest efforts ever.

Everywhere, the crowds gathered, quiet, thoughtful, interested, quickly and easily stirred to laughter, thickening during the day until by early afternoon London was nearly as full of people as it would be on the day itself.

Carraway's cars were everywhere, but London crowds had seldom been less troubled by expert pickpockets, bag snatchers and petty thieves.

Gideon, at the Yard, went across to look at the river; then heard footsteps outside breaking the Yard's Sabbath quiet. The door opened, and Ripple appeared.

"Hallo, George!"

"Hallo, Rip. Glad you're back."

"How are things?"

"All under control, I think," Gideon said.

"I counted twenty-seven of our chaps at the airport and on the way here," said Ripple. "I hope nothing crops up to cause a distraction."

"And don't I!" said Gideon.

Matthew Smith was waiting almost in anguish for Wednesday: all he could think about was throwing his bomb. Violet Timson was waiting very contentedly for Ricky Wall, who was back in London. By coincidence he had come on the same plane as Ripple. Doris Green was blissfully happy because already Arthur had talked of marriage. Carraway was doing a big business, feeling quite secure; and Eric Little's wife was trying to make her children understand the long wait for their father. Beryl Belman was pleasantly surprised that her mother was already perking up. Sonnley was waiting until the moment came to cut Klein's throat; and Klein was trying to grasp what had hit the Glasgow Blacks, for Jock Gorra was already back home, held for questioning about an old robbery with violence. Klein had virtually nothing to do, had no money and no goods to collect and sell—and he knew now that Sonnley would be out to get him if he once suspected the truth. Parsons was waiting for a chance to send the Italian procurer out of the country, with some of his beauties, but giving up hope—and the security officers from the four great countries could hardly wait to get the Visit over.

19

ARRIVALS

ON THAT crucial Monday, the skies were clear, there was a zephyr wind of six miles an hour, and near-perfect visibility. London went about its normal business, shouldering aside the inconvenience near the Procession route, where the hammering took on a more urgent note, and sightseers from out of town and overseas began to give even dingy streets a festive look.

One after another, the aircraft with their important passengers flew in, landed quite trouble-free, and emptied. Britain's Queen and her consort, the Prime Minister and the Foreign Secretary, were there to greet them. Sleek cars rolled along the highways leading to the city. Crowds were thin at first, with groups of children gathered in wide places, waving flags of four nations; cheering, eager, showing hope and faith in the world that these men were trying to fashion.

Nearer the heart of London, the crowds grew thicker and the cheering louder; but it soon faded as the cars stopped at embassies and hotels, their passengers stepped out, paused again for cameras and flashlights, then disappeared to relax for a while, and to gear themselves for the first of the great occasions.

The great occasion would be Wednesday's Procession.

On the Tuesday, late in the afternoon, Sir Reginald Scott-Marle stood up from the end of the large table in the Conference Room, and looked at the group assembled there: Rogerson, Gideon, Ripple, Cox, Mollet, Bayer, Webron and Donnelly, the British Head of Immigration, and Mullivany, the Yard's secretary. Mullivany had sat throughout the last hour, listening to the final plans and the up-to-the-minute reports without a word of complaint or disapproval.

"Everyone is satisfied, then," said Scott-Marle. "Apparently we all have reason to be. I shall be available in the morning until ten o'clock, an hour before the Procession leaves the Palace. If there is any kind of emergency or anxiety, call on me." His voice, his way of barely moving his lips when he spoke, added a curious emphasis. "Now shall we adjourn to my office for a drink?"

He turned round, and the door leading to his office was opened by a youthful-looking man; beyond, the bottles and glasses were on a table by the window. The sun was shining on the bottles, firing them with a hundred colours.

Ripple followed Gideon through the doorway.

"It will be over tomorrow, thank God."

"We'll just be clearing up the mess," said Gideon, and added under his breath: "I hope."

When Gideon got back to his office, after the cocktails, he sat on a corner of his desk and ran through reports that had come in. One was from Lemaitre:

"All the Glasgow boys have gone home, George. Bob's your Uncle!"

Gideon grinned.

Another report said that there was no indication as to where the soil heaped up in a suburban garden had come from. The Divisional Superintendent simply said: "Will check when opportunity arises," and Gideon decided that it was not worth too much trouble.

"We can check that when the rush is over," he said to Bell.

"Rush? What rush?" asked Bell.

Gideon laughed, thought warmly of Bell, and then lifted a telephone: "Get Mrs. Gideon for me," he said, and sat swinging his leg. There was an empty sense of anticlimax now that so much was over, and the persistent feeling of uneasiness had no specific cause. The trouble was that he had nothing active to do, and he needed action.

Bell had gone home early.

The call was a long time coming through, which probably meant that Kate was out.

"Mrs. Gideon, sir."

"Hallo, Kate," Gideon said. "Like to know something hard to believe?"

"You're not coming home tonight," said Kate philosophically.

"I'm free now. Care to come up, and have a stroll along the route? I'm told they're gathering pretty thick already."

Kate began : "I promised Priscilla I would—"

"She home?"

"They're all home."

"Bring 'em all up," said Gideon expensively. "I'll lay on a meal somewhere."

"No, don't do that, it'll be hopeless getting a meal out tonight," said Kate. She was obviously pleased. "You get something at the Yard, and we'll have a snack here and be in Whitehall at nine o'clock. Is that all right?"

"Couldn't be better," said Gideon.

At five past nine, he saw Kate, Priscilla, Penelope and young Malcolm, all hurrying because they were a few minutes late, all looking eager and fresh, Malcolm leading the way through the crowd, the girls behind him, Kate bringing up the rear, a head taller than any of them. A lot of men looked at the Gideon girls and as many took notice of Kate.

They met at the corner of Parliament Street and Parliament Square ; Kate and Gideon touched hands, and then they began to move among the crowds thronging the square, and walked · back along Whitehall past the thousands of people who planned to sleep out all night.

It was warm, the weather forecast was good, more and more people were streaming along, and the front seats were already taken. Rubber cushions, little stools, air-beds, all of these gadgets and a hundred others were in use. The crowd was high-spirited and good-tempered. A crowd of young Australians had a spot nearly opposite Downing Street, and were shouting exchanges with a smaller crowd of French students, and some middle-aged Americans.

"I ain't done such a thing as this in my whole life," a woman said, with a Southern drawl. "But nobody's going to stop me tonight, Jim. I'm staying right here."

"You do just that, *Maaaaam*," an Australian mimicked.

The Gideons reached the narrow stretch of pavement in front of the stand where Kate would be next day. The pavement here was crowded, but only one row of all-nighters was allowed on the kerb. Gideon took no special notice of them.

Malcolm Gideon actually stepped over Matthew Smith's legs.

The programme sellers, the sellers of cardboard and cheap mirror periscopes, the souvenir pedlars, were out in their hundreds, and Gideon wondered how much of the stuff being offered had been stolen. There were reports of a strained relationship between Sonnley and Klein, but crooks had been known to use a quarrel as a smoke-screen, and if anything it made Gideon more suspicious. He saw pound notes and ten-shilling notes changing hands freely, for London crowds were always free with their money on nights like these.

He saw Donnelly and Webron, on the other side of Whitehall; they waved. There was no sign of Mollet or Bayer, but as he reached the Mall he saw Parsons, on his own, looking like an evangelist. Gideon felt Kate's hand touching his. Some Australian detectives were in the Mall, but Wall wasn't among them. The Mall was already jammed tight with people.

Near the Palace, Gideon saw Ripple, mingling with the crowd; they exchanged glances, but otherwise did not acknowledge each other.

20

GREAT DAY

LONDON stirred . . .

Along the route of the morning's procession, Londoners
woke in their thousands after the long, uneasy night,
cramped, stiff, hungry, unwashed, unshaven, bleary-eyed,
dour at first, but quick to find good humour.

The trek to the toilets began. The trek of the hawkers
and barrow boys, the programme sellers, the souvenir
sellers, began. The cameras began to click, for the sun had
risen early and the sky was a clear blue : the unbelievable
perfect day. It was warm at six o'clock, warmer at seven,
getting quite hot by nine o'clock; but long before then the
crowds were thronging in from the suburbs. The extra
buses were carrying massive loads; the unseen, unheard
tubes were running through London's bowels, and dis-
gorging passengers from the stations at Westminster
Bridge, Piccadilly, Charing Cross and Trafalgar Square,
at Victoria, Dover Street and St. James's. Scarlet buses
dropped their passengers as near to the Procession route
as they were allowed to go; and masses walked across the
bridges, the young hop-skipping-and-jumping, many
parents flagging already, the middle-aged and the elderly
showing a curious earnestness.

This was a great occasion, one of London's great days,
second only to a Coronation.

The restaurants open for special breakfasts were
crowded, and long queues waited outside them. The
coffee bars could not serve lukewarm coffee and stale buns
fast enough.

The scene along the Mall was at once so familiar, and
yet so strange, that visitors from overseas were baffled and
bewildered by the packed throng, the masses of paper used

overnight as sheets, the mess, the muddle, the good temper, the colour, the drabness, the bare arms, the men's shirt-sleeves.

And out of London's Divisions came the uniformed policemen, to relieve those who had been on duty all night.

In the Information Room, Gideon and Cox followed their movements as the Units reported.

They came from the perimeter of London and all the outer Divisions, in black marias, in buses and in coaches. Each policeman carried his shiny rolled cape because England's June could not be trusted. Each man was dressed in heavy dark blue, each helmeted, each was already hot, slow-walking, firm-footed, quite unperturbed by the occasion, knowing that his job was as much to keep the crowd in humour as to keep them in order; the contented crowd would offer little trouble.

The police walked in their dozens, in twenties, in thirties and forties, under the command of sergeants from the central Divisions. They took up their places along the route, in front of the crowds, standing quite close to one another. The ribaldry began to flow from the people behind towards the policemen, who stood at ease and joked among themselves, but did not tempt fate by answering back the civilians.

"Perfect job, your chaps," Gideon said, and Cox smiled mechanically.

Then came the first of the troops, from the Navy, the Army, the Air Force: battalions of them marching in military precision to the places *en route* which they must line; heels clicking, arms swinging, more unbending then the police, obeying barrack-square voice orders, some looking a little apprehensively up at the sky. If it didn't cloud over before long, it was going to be stinking hot, and hours standing under this gruelling heat was no one's idea of a joke. They talked in asides, ignoring the banter of the crowd. Horns honked on the outskirts.

The Special Branch and C.I.D. men mingled with the crowd. All the windows on the buildings were watched.

In each of the buildings officials checked that no un-
authorized person got in. Men from the Special Branch
climbed up through skylights to the roofs, and some took
up positions which they would hold all day. The television
and newsreel cameras were at their various vantage points,
click, click, clicking in practice runs.

Big Ben boomed out, impersonally, resonantly. The sun
rose higher. The prospects of the hawkers grew less, but
they were well satisfied, many already packing up and
going home; but the newspaper sellers were out in force.
The pigeons in Trafalgar Square had a forlorn and
neglected air; their turn would come when the crowds
started to move again. Now only a few children fed them
corn, and few cameras clicked at them.

At Wellington Barracks the Guards foregathered : the
Horse Guards, the Household Cavalry, the Life Guards.
The big, black horses were saddled and bridled; collar
chain, breastplates and sheepskin were checked; all that
was metal gleamed and glittered. The men were mar-
shalled, medals shimmering and plumes erect as a fox's
brush, tunics tight across packed shoulders and deep
chests, pouch belts looking as if they were powdered with
unmelted snow, white breeches stiff as with starch or pipe-
clay, spurs glistening behind the jackboots, forever a threat
but never to be used on the flanks of the big black horses.
The gauntlet gloves were pulled on firmly; each state
sword was held fast by its white sling.

The orders rang out.

The Guards moved into position, as if horses and men
were moved by the same reflexes and the same impulses,
and they rode along the Birdcage Walk towards the
Palace, where the State Coach and the Coaches for the
Heads of States had been waiting—with Security Police
from all four countries watching surreptitiously, looking
for anything which was even slightly amiss.

Huge crowds, gathered on the steps and the fountain
opposite the Palace, broke into cheers before they were
due. People laughed and shouted and chattered and eased
cramped muscles. Time ticked slowly by until the first

roar went up as a row of police from the Mounted Branch led by their Inspector clattered out of the Palace gates and clip-clopped smartly up the Mall and along the whole route; to clear the way, to tell their colleagues on the sides and among the trees, at the roofs and at the windows, that all was well further along the route, and that the Procession would soon start in earnest. The police riders looked straight ahead, winning some cheers touched with irony, as many with admiration, bringing cracks from the crowd to the standing uniformed men—*"Didn't your mother teach you to ride a horse, Charley?"* or *"Mind he don't bite you, Bert,"* or *"When are we going to see the real thing?"* But it wouldn't be long, now, and the crowd knew it. There was a kind of tension among them all; faces were turned right or left, towards the direction from which the first of the Cavalry would come.

Suddenly there was a great roar of cheering as the golden coach appeared in the Palace yard, the clattering guards in front and behind it, a figure in gold-coloured satin sitting on one side, the Duke in his uniform as Admiral of the Fleet on the other.

Now the deep-throated cheers rose in waves along the Mall, and the periscopes went up. The tall and the tiny went on tiptoe, fathers lifted pleading children, and the cries of protest came. *"Expect me to see through your blooming head?"* Small feet kicked against stiff shoulders and chests, the lucky six-footers stood at the back, looking disdainfully over the masses of heads. The troops lining the route clicked to the salute as the royal carriage drew near, and then the other Heads of State, first the American, then the French, then the German . . .

The Special Branch and C.I.D. men were keyed up, even the most experienced of them tight-lipped and hard-eyed, watching, watching for any trifling tell-tale sign of danger. The men from the four countries were with their English colleagues now, watching, hopeful, admiring; still a little anxious, in case the one thing they could not prevent should come about. A shot *could* ring out; a fool *might* try to rush towards the carriages.

But nothing happened to alarm them. The Queen's Guard rode by in sun-bathed splendour, the gilt of the coaches and the beauty of the dresses, the radiance of the Queen, the calmness of her consort, the massive elegance of the President of France, the tall, slim figure of the President of the United States in a morning suit, the President of West Germany, liked a carved figure from the Black Forest, face unsmiling.

The Procession was at its height.

The coach in which the President of France and his lady rode turned out of Admiralty Arch towards the Houses of Parliament.

Gideon was now in his office with Cox, a more relaxed Cox, watching a television picture of the corner of Parliament Street and Parliament Square, so he had a bird's-eye view of all this pomp and panoply. His anxieties were drawn out of him by the beauty and the splendour, and by the thought of the hopes which mankind based on this one day.

Further along, in the House of Lords, that golden chamber, the members of both Houses were waiting. The police who protected Parliament were on duty at the gates, and what happened once the coaches were through was no direct concern of Gideon's. If there were to be trouble he believed it would be on the way in—any time, now; any moment. But there had been hundreds of processions before; he himself had taken part in dozens; and there had been no serious trouble at any, yet, no single act of madness.

He saw a picture of the stand where Kate was sitting, very glad that she was there. Malcolm was somewhere among the crowds; the two girls had stayed away. Then he frowned. The pavement in front of the stand was jammed tight with people, although he had ordered two lines only. He glanced at Cox, and saw Cox's face suddenly pale and drawn, saw his hands clench.

"I—" began Cox, and gulped. "I forgot to order that pavement clear. I—God!" He was sweating.

"It won't do any harm," Gideon reassured him quickly. "Bound to have something go a bit wrong. It's been near perfect. Forget it."

He saw a little man in front of the stand, the very front. Then he looked at Kate again.

Kate Gideon was watching with a feeling almost of enchantment, like most of the women in the stand. About her were the Americans, the French, the Germans, the Indians, the Africans—people from all countries and all continents, with huge cameras or with small cameras, now whirring, now clicking. Some people were silent, watching, holding their breath, eyes strained to get the nearest vision of the Queen. Glasses pressed tight against a thousand eyes, the magnified figures showing something of the radiance.

Kate looked her fill at the Queen, who seemed younger at each of these great occasions, and then watched the Household Cavalry clattering and clicking behind. She saw the white horses of the coach in which the President of the United States was sitting; after that would come the President of France. His carriage would be here in two or three minutes. The whole procession would not last for more than seven or eight, but every second was well worth while.

Rosie Sonnley was in the stand, sucking peppermints. Cox's wife was there, within waving distance of Kate. Doris Green sat with her hand in Arthur's, warm and snug. She knew how much older he was, but it did not seem to matter to her; this was like a golden dream. They sat behind two empty seats, with a wonderful view.

Detective-Inspector Ricky Wall, of the Sydney C.I.D., was sitting half-way down the stand, actually on the steps, to allow a little woman next to him to get a better view. Just below him was Donnelly. Webron was somewhere in the Mall. A place where Lemaitre was to have been on duty was vacant, but few noticed that. Wall felt the kind of emotional excitement which he had thought himself proof against; he saw Donnelly wave his hands, and thought he heard his cheers, as the President of the United States went by, completely self-assured, his lovely wife perhaps a little over-awed.

Donnelly, still cheering, saw a man sitting on the kerb open a small case and take out a vacuum flask. That seemed so odd at such a moment that Donnelly stared.

The man Donnelly noticed was at the front, and must have been there all night, but when the cheering was at its height, when the moment was supreme, he was taking out a vacuum flask! Wall watched him closely, too.

Donnelly saw that the man did not unscrew the top, but held the flask by his side. He would not have been able to see so clearly, but the police had kept the road itself clear, and there was a gap where a party of children stood. Why take out a flask at such a moment? And why take out a flask at any time and not pour out?

Then Donnelly remembered talking to Ripple about a bomb disguised as a vacuum flask, captured from Algerian extremists. Donnelly jumped up and ran down the steps, then saw Gideon's *aide*, Joe Bell, on the street corner near the man. To shout would be a waste of time.

Donnelly vaulted over the front of the stand, by the steps; a woman cried out, but her voice was drowned. The nearest soldier swung round to face the crowd. Donnelly landed on the pavement. Bell saw the movement out of the corner of his eyes, swung round, and recognized the American. Bell came pushing his way through the thick crowd, cursing the fact that the pavement here hadn't been kept clear.

"What is it?"

"Look at that guy!" Donnelly shouted close to his ear. "The man with the flask!"

The French coach was coming now, the clip-clop-clip of the horses' hooves sharp and clear, the coachmen holding the reins as if born to it. The President was bowing, his wife smiling and inclining her head. Cheers from the crowd of French students rose in wild waves, then they swung into the first bars of the *Marseillaise*. Bell turned to see the little man in crumpled clerical grey holding the flask in his hand. He raised his hand high, then drew his arm back, as would any man who was going to throw.

The people alongside him were too anxious to see the procession to take any notice, and the soldiers were watching Wall, Bell and Donnelly.

Bell roared: *"Stop that!"* and sprang forward. The little man must have heard him, for he half-turned, arm drawn right back, the flask tight in pale, thin fingers. Bell was only two yards from him, when the man swung round and hurled the flask into the air. As he did so, a guardsman saw the danger, stuck his rifle forward, and caught Matthew Smith on the forearm. Instead of going towards the President of France, the flask rose high into the air, then curved more quickly down towards the front of the stand, behind Smith.

Smith began to kick and struggle. Bell put a hammerlock on him, thrusting his arm up, and saw the flask dropping downwards. For an awful moment he thought that it would fall into the stand. He let the prisoner go, and flung himself towards the falling object. Another C.I.D. man came running, but was too far away to help.

The flask hit the front of the stand.

Bell saw the white flash, and it blinded him; heard the roar, and was deafened. On the instant, he felt as if his body had been ripped into pieces. Immediately behind him were two empty seats—and behind them a man and a young girl; Doris Green with her lover. A piece of metal smashed into her forehead, killing her instantly. Another gashed Arthur Ritter's left eye; he died before the police reached him.

Out on the road, horses reared up, startled heads turned; people began to scream.

Watching, with horrified fascination, Gideon could hardly think at first. Then he realized that the carriages were not damaged, the worst had not happened. It was terrible, dreadful, but—

"My God!" he breathed. "Kate."

He searched among the faces on the screen, transfixed with a deeper sense of horror, until suddenly he caught sight of her, talking to Ray Cox's wife.

For a few minutes that relief seemed to ease the shock of Bell.

21

DAY'S END

"The bomb hit the front of the stand, which took the brunt of the explosion, and Bell took the rest," said Donnelly to Gideon, when everything was over. "I think he thought if he could smother it with his body he would save a lot of lives. Two others were killed, and a dozen hurt, but none of the injured are too bad. The man who threw the bomb is over at Cannon Row, gibbering. He's the nearest thing to crazy I've ever seen. It seems as if the failure drove him round the bend."

Donnelly looked sick and pale. So did Wall, who was with them.

"If it hadn't been for sheer luck, I'd have been there," he said. "So would half a dozen of us. We'd have been goners, too."

Cox caught his breath, and Gideon glanced at him, nodded understanding of his great relief, and then asked : "Was anyone else in the stand hurt?"

"No, except a few cuts," Donnelly said.

Gideon was sitting at his desk, and looking across at Bell's desk, and the chair which would never be Bell's again. That was the hardest thing to realize. The death of Bell affected him more, at the moment, than the fact that there had been an attempted assassination.

Ripple was with Rogerson and Mollet, and the Commissioner was on his way back. The Heads of State were in the Gilded Chamber. Except for that one little patch of horror now cordoned off, everything in London was normal, although rumours of what had happened were spreading fast.

One of Gideon's telephones rang. At moments like these it had been Bell's habit to lift his extension, and make sure

that his boss wasn't harassed unnecessarily. *Joe, Joe, Joe.*
Gideon lifted the telephone and said :

"Gideon."

"Now the show's over, I can tell you something," a man
said. It was Lemaitre. "I've picked up some of Sonnley's
boys flashing phoney fivers about. We've made four
arrests, and they all say that Benny Klein gave them the
money. Shall I pick up Benny?"

Gideon said : "Get him, but have someone else do it,
Lem. I need you here."

Cox looked at him, and saw how drawn his face was;
and realized what a terrible blow Bell's death was to him.
Yet this man had thought to glance reassuringly at him
because of the ironic good consequences of that forgotten
order. Cox felt suddenly very humble, but it was a long
time before he realized just what the emotion was.

Soon Lemaitre came in, followed by Mollet and Ripple.
Mollet just raised his hands, and went to the window.
Lemaitre said :

"Queer thing, George."

"What is ?"

"The assassin's a chap named Smith—there was a
report about his wife being missing. Remember? Some
digging done in the garden."

"I remember."

"The digging was under the floor of a workshop in the
garden; his wife was there."

Gideon said : "Good God." He closed his eyes for a
moment, and then said : "You tried, Ray—God knows
you tried that one."

Mollet turned round.

"This assassin—when will he be charged?" he asked.

"This afternoon," replied Gideon. "We'll hold a special
court. Why?"

"I would like to be able to give Paris the latest information," said Mollet. "I will telephone." He went out,
still badly shaken, and Ripple and Cox went with him;
Gideon saw Ripple glance at Bell's desk as he went out.

Lemaitre was on the telephone, giving instructions about Sonnley, and Gideon said to Donnelly and Wall :

"Going back to the route for the return procession?"

"I don't want any more of that," said Wall. "I had a bellyful."

"Go and see if Miss Timson's free, will you?" Gideon asked. "If she is, ask her to lay on a car for me at once, my own's not here. I want to go and see Mrs. Bell." He noticed the alacrity with which the Australian went out, but there was no brightness in his own eyes or lightness in his heart when he looked across at Lemaitre.

And Lemaitre, after a moment's hesitation, deliberately sat down in Bell's chair; the chair Lemaitre had occupied for several years before Bell had taken on this job—the job that had killed him.

"Lem," said Gideon, his throat dry, "how about Sonnley's shops?"

Donnelly said : "I'll be seeing you."

"Clean as a whistle," reported Lemaitre. "I've checked with four Divisions. Might have some stolen stuff, but there's nothing we can pin on to them for certain. They look as clean as—*hey*! Think Sonnley's fixed Klein? Blimey!" went on Lemaitre, and gave a choky kind of laugh. "We'll get the pair of them. Klein will squeal all right."

There was a tap at the door as he finished, and Abbott came in. It was difficult to define the change in Abbott, but it was there—as if the Carraway case had forged a kind of steel in him.

"If Carraway had any part in the murders of his partner and of Marjorie Belman, he'll get away with it this time," Abbott said. "I think we ought to go it alone, and charge Little with the girl's murder."

"Right," said Gideon. "I'll talk to the Public Prosecutor. Anything else, Lem?"

"Anything special you want me to do?"

"Pass all your current jobs on to someone else, and take over Joe's desk, will you?" Gideon said quietly. "We're going to need a lot of help today, this bloody thing won't stop—"

A telephone bell began to ring.

One or the other kept ringing, and it wasn't until nearly one o'clock that a call which Gideon was waiting for came through.

It was Christy, of N.E., brisk to a point of brusquesness, and hard-voiced.

"I've heard about Joe Bell, George."

Gideon said : "I suppose you have."

"I can't say—"

"Hugh," Gideon interrupted harshly, "have you got Klein?"

After a long pause, Christy said : "Yes. Picked him up with five thousand pounds in new pound notes. They're so good that our expert can't swear whether they're real or false, except by the tintometer—the ink's the wrong colour. No doubt about it, he says. Klein swears that Sonnley gave him the money, but Sonnley says he doesn't know a thing about it. He says he knows Klein just sold him out to Gorra, why should he pay him anything? I doubt if we'll get Sonnley this time."

"His day will come," Gideon said heavily.

He was heavy-hearted all the time he was in his office, and he was there until after nine o'clock.

Outside, London was still noisily awake, thronging the procession route, traipsing over the carpets of old newspapers littering the ground, the litter and the debris of the crowd.

The President's escape did little to soften the impact of Bell's death ; Ripple too took it badly to heart. Miss Timson worked very late that night, because there had been a hitch in the plans for the flight back to Australia of the touring detectives. How would the future work out for her? Did Australia really beckon?

Gideon checked the arrangements for the hearing against Little, looked over the report of the brief proceedings in which Matthew Smith had been charged with using an explosive to the public danger and remanded in custody. The court had been so crowded that even Mollet had had difficulty in getting in.

Gideon drove home about ten o'clock, and the front door opened as he pulled up outside. He recalled Joe Bell's wife, short, dumpy, fluffy, shocked to a stupor of silence. When Kate came towards him, hands outstretched, his eyes stung. He felt very tired—but at least the Visit was nearly over.

THE END